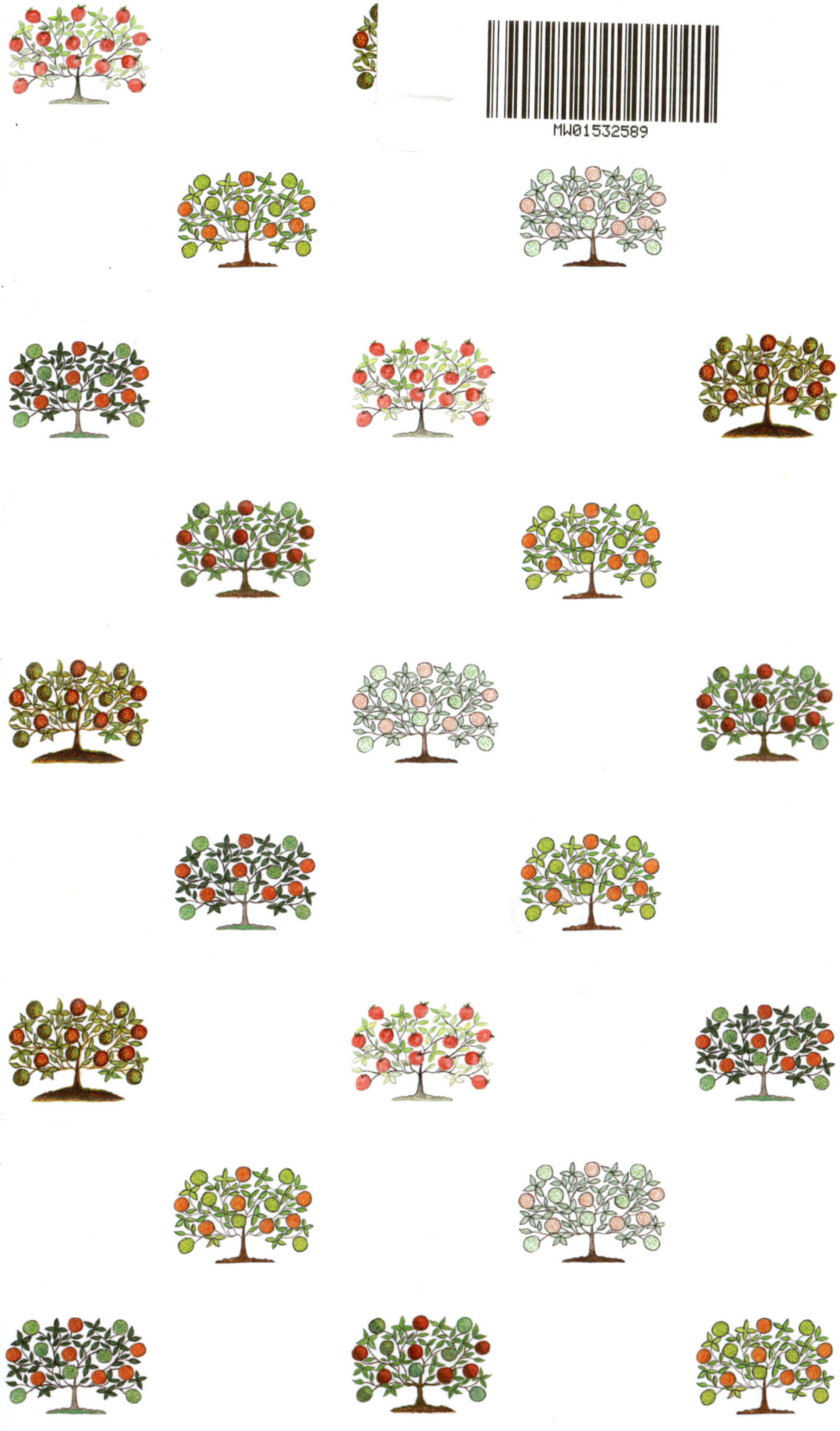

Creative Elders

ORIGINAL STORIES, POEMS AND REFLECTIONS

SHAKER POINTE COMMUNITY RESIDENTS

CREATIVE ELDERS
ORIGINAL STORIES, POEMS, AND REFLECTIONS

Project Manager:
Ann M. Krupski

Book Designer:
Laurie Musick Wright, LMW Design

Cover Illustration:
Jack Egan (1942-2021)

Photos and illustrations throughout provided by
Shaker Pointe and the contributors.
Photos with no credit line are licensed from stock.adobe.com.
Contributor photos by Enchanted Reflections Photography.

Printed in the United States of America by Troy Book Makers
ISBN: 978-1-61468-793-1

TABLE OF CONTENTS

PREFACE

Shaker Pointe is an independent living retirement community in Latham, New York. In the ten years I have lived here, I have seen creativity thrive. Examples are abundant: violinists in local orchestras; singing in harmony, including in a local gospel group; musical composition – instrumental and vocal; stunning art work; amazing nature photography; beautiful raised bed gardens; generous volunteering at local agencies; caring outreach to neighbors; organized collections of donations for those in need.

Creativity continues to flourish, long after traditional retirement from work. There are numerous accomplishments possible that are valuable for ourselves and others. This collection of writings radiates that reality. Those who have contributed to this volume are between the ages of 69 and 96.

A spirit of adventure prevailed as we participated in the mystery, joys and challenges of our creative endeavors. We have been amazed along the way and are delighted to share our creative accomplishments. We applaud any efforts in a similar engagement wherever retirees live together.

— Ann M. Krupski

Ronnie Uss, Shaker Pointe at Carondelet

SHAKER POINTE ANTHOLOGY
— By Paul Grondahl

I work with a lot of young, aspiring authors and my goal is to help them overcome their procrastination at getting started, face down the blank page, build their self-confidence and convince them that they are writers with something worth saying through their prose.

I have worked with writers from age eight to ninety-eight and the common theme that cuts across the generations is this: they don't feel they have anything worth writing and, even if they did, they lack the skills to express it.

To that I say phooey – or, actually, something much stronger and profane.

Everyone can be a writer and everyone has a story worth telling. My experience across four decades as a journalist, author and teacher has convinced me of that fact. I know it in my bones.

When I visited Shaker Pointe in June 2022 for a writing workshop, I encountered a few of the same, old excuses. Here were a group of seniors, many of whom were old enough to be my parents, and they suffered from some of the same sense of self-doubt and writerly hang-ups as high school students with whom I have worked. There is no age requirement on a fear of writing.

Yet, as the morning workshop at Shaker Pointe progressed and residents began to read and share their work, I was pleasantly surprised at what I observed. Here was a group of committed writers who took their writing seriously and who moved well beyond the trials and tribulations of the novice. We listened intently to each other's work, offered critiques and constructive criticism, made suggestions for editing. We engaged in a lively discussion of what we thought worked well and what did not in each piece presented. A group of seasoned storytellers emerged.

I especially enjoyed the sense of camaraderie and collaboration among the writing workshop participants. There was a generous spirit to the process, of wanting to encourage and lift each other up in the course of making practical editorial suggestions. In short, I felt like I was becoming part of a caring, supportive community of writers.

I know from my own experience that the aging process — and the reality of outliving spouses, family members and friends — can leave a person feeling lonely and isolated. The community of writers at Shaker Pointe is an antidote to any sense of aloneness. They have a shared passion and a common purpose.

Which brings me to their anthology, this collection of poems, essays, fiction and reminiscences written by residents of Shaker Pointe. What a wonderful idea. I am so glad that they are following through and publishing this volume.

We critiqued many of these pieces in our workshop and I

was impressed by the level of their writing skills and their obvious commitment to honing their writing craft. There are too many works to single out any individually, but I enjoyed the depth and breadth of the offerings. Some are heartfelt tributes, in memoriam pieces written to celebrate a lost loved one. Others are nostalgic reminiscences of a time and place that no longer exists. Others are examples of creative expression using fictionalized characters and stories. There are a number of poems that range from funny to sad, from profound meditations on the meaning of life to simple observations of the natural world.

They are all so different, so original, and as unique as a fingerprint. They showcase each writer's distinct style and an authentic voice. The Shaker Pointe community of writers underscore for me the fact that everyone is a writer with something important to say.

It was my honor to work with them, to get to know them, and to reconnect with some friends that I have known over the years. It is wonderful that they are publishing this anthology and that it is a gift they can share with their children, grandchildren, great-grandchildren and friends. It is a legacy project, one that will remain for generations in bookcases and on shelves in libraries and homes across the Capital Region and beyond. When they write the history of Shaker Pointe, the anthology will be a reference point that captures a sense of place and the spirit of its residents.

A quote from English author E.M. Forster in his 1910 novel *Howards End* comes to mind: "Only connect! That was the whole of her sermon. Only connect the prose and the passion, and both will be exalted, and human love will be seen at its height. Live in fragments no longer."

That quote is apropos to this published anthology and all of those at Shaker Pointe who contributed to its publication as writers, editors, publishers and production assistants.

Bravo to all of them. This book is the fruit of their labor. I hope it continues. I hope they publish more anthologies, perhaps make it an annual Shaker Pointe tradition. It represents the culmination of a community of authors who worked together for the common good, who supported each other, and who discovered that writing can be rewarding.

I would be remiss if I did not offer a special thanks to Ann Krupski, who invited me to lead the writing workshop and who was a driving force behind the anthology project. Ann is a wonderful poet whose poem, "Connections," is part of this anthology. It captures the mood of connectedness among everyone who contributed to this project and the feeling she describes of "a spontaneous, shared warmth with another."

Bravo to the writers of Shaker Pointe. Congratulations on this first published anthology. May there be many more.

The Tree of Life

The Tree of Life is an ancient, universal symbol of the vibrancy of life. The Shaker Tree of Life, attributed to Hannah Cohoon (1788 -1864), is an especially vivid depiction, with its bold red and green colors.

In 2008, the Shaker Pointe community chose the Shaker Tree of Life as its logo. Pictures of this tree rendered by some of our residents are found in this book.

ShakerPointe

AT CARONDELET

CREATIVE ELDERS

CHAPTER ONE

Fiction

TREE OF LIFE: Nancy Scarchilli

Ted Zborowski, "Swallowtail"

THE MAY 15 GLASS

Vince Powers

It was May 15, 1820. Thomas Jefferson was sitting in his study, playing with that piece of glass. Still puzzling over it. Sunday, the day before, Rev. Frederick Hatch, the Episcopalian pastor down in Charlottesville, had come up to Monticello for a service for the Jefferson household. After the service, at breakfast, Thomas had shown the glass to the clergyman and asked his opinion. The man was well educated and might have some insight. But nothing came of it.

Thomas had already sought opinions from everyone in the house, family members and house slaves. Like Thomas himself, no one knew what to think of it.

The previous Saturday was a slow day, and he had had some time to do something he had been thinking of. He took a small piece of glass that he had in the house, and heated it until it was white hot, handled only with tools so his hands didn't get destroyed. When glass is that hot, it becomes very malleable, and can be twisted and pulled into any shape the handler wants. He wanted to shape it like a sine wave, and he did. The S-shaped sine wave was being much talked about in mathematics at the time. Mathematically, it can be used to represent anything that changes with regularity, such as sound, and Thomas had recently become interested in it.

Thomas did some reading while he waited patiently for the glass to cool, so he could pick it up with his bare hands and

17

examine it. When he finally did so, it felt like glass always feels, hard and smooth. But something was wrong. The glass was flexible. Very flexible. He could bend it and twist it any way he wanted. Then, when he released it, the glass at once returned to the shape he had given it, the sine wave shape. Glass does not behave like that. It is not flexible at normal temperatures. So why was this piece flexible?

By Monday, Thomas had exhausted his efforts. He had obtained no thoughts, no opinions, from anyone. His own strongest speculation was that the piece of glass he used was made with some alien substance in it that gave the glass this bizarre property. He had no idea where the glass had come from and asking all the house slaves and even garden slaves provided no clues.

That night, Thomas wrote about it in his journal. He decided to refer to it as "The May 15 Glass," taking the current date as the name.

The May 15 Glass remains a mystery because it has never been found. No one in his household ever knew what happened to it. Jefferson never referred to it again in his multiple writings. And none of his friends are known to have said Jefferson told them about it. Did it really exist? Did Jefferson really discover this odd piece of glass, or did he somehow imagine it because of an unknown influence? Or did he write about it as a joke? A mystery of history.

THE WRITER AND BEN

Vince Powers

Ben hesitated, thinking. Did he really want to go into that room? But then he decided. I may never know the truth unless I do. He turned to his left and started walking.

I think I'll sit down here, and maybe start reading my book again. Wait! Why am I walking? I don't want to go anywhere. What's going on, my feet are acting on their own!

At the door to the room, Ben paused and looked around. He didn't see anything at first glance. He decided to look more carefully before he entered the room. Make sure as best he can that he doesn't miss something.

Okay, now I've stopped. So, feet, pay more attention. I didn't want to walk. You finally got it. So let's go back to the chair so I can read. Well, c'mon feet, do it! Start walking to go back there. What in the world is happening here, that my feet won't do what I want them to? First, they walked when I didn't want them to. Now I want them to walk, and they won't.

Ben more carefully scanned the room, looking at every inch attentively. And still, he almost missed it. Almost, but not quite. There, under that side table. What's that? He slowly made his way to the table, with his eyes fixed on what was under the table.

*Wait, I'm starting to walk again. My feet **are** working, just slow to respond. Oh, no – I'm walking, but in the wrong direction. Feet, not that way! What's going on?*

I'm getting an idea in my head, and I don't like it. Maybe that writer is doing something again. He was at it yesterday. And things were happening to me that I didn't like. I was doing things I didn't want to do. Sorta like now, though yesterday it wasn't about walking. Can that writer be doing something to me? How would that even be possible? Mental telepathy or something?

Ben stooped down to look at the object. Yes, it was exactly what he thought it might be, the missing key. How did it get here? He knew for certain that he did not go into this room when he got home last night. He came into the house, locked the door, turned out the light and went upstairs. He remembered it all very clearly. So how did the key get here?

Why did I just stoop down and reach under the side table? I'm sure it's that writer again! I've got to find a way to stop him from making me do things. I'm not a slave, after all. I don't have to do whatever he wants, just because he wants it.

Ben needed to think about what is going on here. The key didn't move itself. A mouse certainly didn't move it; that's a crazy idea. There's no one else in the house, so another person didn't move it. He walked out to the room he had just come from and sat down to think.

Okay, now I'm moving again. I didn't decide to, my feet just started to walk. It's like my feet have a mind of their own, independent of mine. Where am I going? Oh, here I am back where I started, and now I'm sitting in the chair. That's what I was going to do five minutes ago! I was going to sit here and read, but I'm not going to read now. I feel too jangled to relax and read now.

I'm convinced now, it's that writer. Whatever he's doing, he's controlling me. It happened yesterday, too. I've got to figure out how to stop him. Can I resist when he's making me do something? Like, when he's making me walk, can I refuse to walk? I'm going to try it! Otherwise, I'm just his robot or something. I wonder if I can resist.

Could it be that I was sleep-walking, and brought the key to the other room? I've never sleep-walked before. At least, not that I know of. I always thought that was the stuff of fiction stories: a man walks in his sleep and does something that later, when he's awake, he doesn't remember doing. But what other explanation can there be for that key to be on the floor under that table this morning? I don't really remember what I did with it last night, but every day for months, years even, I always do the same thing: when I come in, I hang the key on its hook next to the door. With such a long-standing habit, I'm sure I did that last night, too.

Hey, how about I right now walk through my actions last night and see if maybe my habit failed me? Yeah, that's what I'll do. He started to rise.

Oops, now I'm trying to stand up. I don't want to do that. The writer is making me. Okay, now's the time to start resisting. I won't stand. Wow, that's hard not to let myself get up! But I've got to do it. He wants me to stand, so I'm going to stay seated, no matter what. Ooh, stay, stay! Don't stand up!

Ben struggled to rise, but just wasn't able to.

It seems to have worked! I'm not trying to stand up anymore! So now I know the writer can't always control me. I can be my own independent self if I want. Good! So, I think I'll …

[AUTHOR'S NOTE. I haven't planned on this scenario. Ben can't stand? I'll stop writing for now, so I can better plan the details of my story.]

All of the above is very strange. Can fictional characters in a writer's story actually have their own consciousness? And have enough of it to refuse to do what the writer wants, at least during the time he's writing? That's what seems to have happened above. Then, when the author stopped writing, the unwilling character disappeared. Is all that possible?

The writer is writing a scene from his larger story. And in the scene, his character is trying to locate a missing key. But his character refuses to cooperate. And the writer doesn't know what to do about it.

Here's what I think. Instead of being a real problem, maybe it's merely another case of what is commonly called Writer's Block. Consider – the writer can't decide whether to develop the sleepwalking idea or go with another yet-to-be-thought-of idea for solving the character Ben's problem; and this fantasy about an uncooperative character pops up. The imaginative writer now has an excuse for not writing,

What do you think?

MY FORTUNE TELLING CAREER

Vince Powers

My name is Cecilia. Last month I found out something cool. My grandfather had spent time tracing the family tree, genealogy he called it, and he told me I was a descendant of a witch. Her name was Mercy Disbrow, and she lived in Connecticut in the 1600s, before there was even a United States. At some point in her life, some people accused her of being a witch, which then was against the law. It was even a capital crime! They put her on trial in 1692 and she was found guilty and condemned to death. But she was not a passive person who gave up easily. While she was in prison waiting to be hung, she filed a lawsuit saying her trial was illegal for some technical reason, having to do with a change of jurors. By the time she got another trial a year later, no one wanted to kill witches anymore, and she was found not guilty and released.

I don't believe Grandma Mercy did all the nutty things she was accused of back then. Anyway, it's okay to be a witch today, thank goodness.

The cool thing is that I'm a witch, too. And nobody is going to have me thrown in jail for it. You know, there aren't too many witches around, so I'm kinda proud to tell people I'm a witch, it makes me stand out.

I've always known I'm a witch. Well, not exactly always. But since 10th grade. My friends and I used to do make-believe séances, and one time I said what would happen in school tomorrow. The next day it happened! My friends all told me then that I was a witch. They actually didn't use the word witch. They said I was a see-er, or seer, because I could see what was going to happen before it did and tell others about it.

Then there was that time I got mad at Jake Schmidt and said, "I wish you would break your leg!" On the way home from school that day, his bike went off the road and his leg was broken! That time, my friends did use the witch word. They said only a witch can put a curse on someone. They actually used the word hex, but I think that's the same thing as a curse.

I recently graduated from high school, and I know I have to find a good job somewhere. I'm still living at home, of course, and mom and dad have never even hinted at me getting a job. But I know the day will come when they will expect me to start making a living for myself. Hey, maybe I can use my witchy powers to predict when that day will come. Then I would be sure to be ready.

I don't know what kind of work I want to do. I can't think of anything I learned in school that will get me a good-paying job. I wonder if I could support myself by being a witch? What do witches do? I've never seen a help wanted ad for a witch. Lots of ads for "Management Trainee" at fast food places; ads for hotel housekeeping ("We Will Train"); assistant at animal shelter. No ads for a witch.

So how can I make a living as a witch? Since I'm a seer, I guess I could open a fortune telling business. I could do tarot cards, because my friends and I in school used to play with tarots, and I learned them then. I could do crystal ball, though I would have to develop a half dozen or so patters. I won't do palm reading, because I don't want to have to learn what all those squiggly lines in your hand are.

I've never actually predicted anything since that one time in 10th grade. But I really have never tried, either. I suppose if I'm going to get a job as a witch, I should practice predicting. How do I do that? And then, how far ahead into the future can I predict? I need to know that, so I can limit my customers to stay within that time frame. So how do I find that out, too?

Yes, I think I will start my own fortune telling business to make a living. What'll I call it? I'm not going to use "Madame" in the name because I'm too young. And besides, I don't like that title anyway. "Cecilia's Fortune Telling?" No, too dull. Maybe "Cecilia Knows All?" That's a lot better – much more power. But maybe drop the word "All" because my witchy powers might be limited, especially right now when I'm first starting out. Yeah, that's it: "Cecilia Knows!" Great name! Let the customers know I can foresee the future, I know what's going to happen. For a price, I'll tell them what it is.

I wonder how I start a fortune telling business? Obviously, I need a place. And a sign or two. I wonder if I need a permit? Do witches or fortune tellers need a permit? Probably. It seems like you need a permit to do anything today. I wonder if you need a permit to be unemployed? Well, whatever, I have to find a way to make a living.

With all these questions I'm asking myself, it's starting to look like I don't know what I'm doing. Well, I sorta don't when it comes to starting my business. Hey, maybe I can get a job as assistant fortune teller someplace and watch how it's all done so then I can do it. Yes! That's what I'll do! Find a fortune teller who needs an assistant and get hired. I bet Google will have some leads.

"Fortune Tellers Near Me." Let Google search for that. Whoa! That's a lot. Hey, look at that. They're called Psychics. Am I a psychic? That sounds like someone who can read minds or something. Is that how they work? They read the client's mind instead of seeing what will happen in the future? I can't read minds. Even if I could, how does that help with telling the future? The client's mind doesn't know the future – that's why they're consulting a fortune teller.

And look: all the blurbs on these psychics' websites talk about them giving "readings." What do they read? Minds? Special secret books? Maybe tarot cards – we used to do that in our get-togethers in school. I could do that kind of reading. Wow, there's a lot more to being a fortune teller —I mean psychic— than I realized.

Well, I've called five psychics to ask if they needed an assistant. Four of them laughed at me and hung up. The fifth one actually talked with me, and what I learned was that the psychic business isn't usually so busy that an assistant is needed.

Then one day the word "intern" popped into my head. I thought "Intern" – maybe that's the way to go. And maybe if I word it right, I can make them feel good about hiring an intern; doctors have interns, rich wealth managers have interns; so, a psychic who has an intern must be somebody very special, and very good at what they do. Yeah, I'll try that.

Later, I actually tried it, and on only the fourth try, a psychic actually told me to come in for an interview! I did. I didn't really have any experience in foretelling, except for that one time in 10th grade, but I did know how to read tarot cards, so he hired me.

The name he used as a psychic was "Rowan." It's a great name, because it speaks of magic and courage and wisdom. There is a tree called the rowan tree, which the Celts sometimes thought of as the tree of life. So, he thought Rowan was a good professional name, and he's been happy with it. He told me what he called a little secret –"don't tell my clients this"– there was a time in Celtic history when the rowan tree berries were thought to be a protection against witchcraft! Ironic! Well, good for him in choosing such a great professional name, but I'm going to stick with my own name, "Cecilia," for now. It's a nice name, and I think a seer could for sure be called Cecilia.

So, the day came when Rowan let me do a reading for a client. He explained to the client that I was his intern, but he had confidence that my reading would be correct and helpful. It did not go well. The first card I turned for the client was The Fool. I told the client I was very sorry to see this card, because it meant that she had been making bad choices for months, and that her life was heading totally in the wrong direction.

The next card was The Hermit. Again, a bad card, I thought. I told the client it meant that she was not trying to change the way she had been doing things, based on those bad choices of hers. She really needs to stop making the same mistakes over and over. Doing that was isolating her from her family and friends, was turning her into an emotional hermit. That's why her family and friends were always telling her to do things she didn't want to do.

I really was hoping for the next card to be good for her. She was already starting to look unhappy and defeated. The card was The World. The World means she wasn't following through on things she needed to do. I tried to think of a good meaning for her. I ended up telling her it was a hopeful sign. It meant that she was starting to make progress toward some of her life goals, and she should keep trying, keep up the good work.

I didn't think the client was very happy about my reading. She certainly didn't look happy. And then Rowan spoke up, and at the same time moved to the center where I was, effectively pushing me aside. He told the client that his intern's reading was good, but not as thorough as it should be. The Fool card did mean she had been making bad decisions, as the intern said, but it also means that she was about to jump away from them and into something much, much better.

He then told the client that The Hermit card was telling her that her solutions were inside her, that if she looked into herself, she would find the seeds of happiness and success.

No longer a need to look to her friends and acquaintances, who were not helping her with their suggestions. Right now, everything she needs is already there inside her. That should make her feel a lot more confident.

Rowan also told her that The World card was a great card for her because it meant that her success was at hand. Good luck and happiness are open to her, just like the world is.

He ended by saying, "Let's draw one more card, to see if all this is true." The card he drew was The Six of Wands. "Wow!" he said. "This is fantastic! You are carrying good karma with you today. This card means you are on the edge of the step to success. In a short time, these problems you brought here today will have disappeared."

I liked his reading, and so did the client. Her appearance had changed from one of defeat to one of courage and defiance. She looked ready to do battle with all the things she was worried about, and win.

I also knew, after hearing his reading for the client, compared to mine, that my internship probably was over. I had almost let that client leave with no success in view and little hope she would see it soon.

Rowan was kind when he told me my internship had ended. He thanked me for the effort, and told me that in his opinion, working as a Psychic was not a career I should pursue. I just didn't have the idea burnt into my psyche that fortune telling, as I called it, required more than trying to tell them what was going to happen. It required an understanding of what a person is feeling at any given moment and making the effort to keep them feeling good about themselves no matter what. In my heart, I knew he was right. I wasn't even thinking about the client when I did the reading. I was thinking about myself and trying to show I knew tarot. I don't think I even knew you were supposed to put yourself in the client's mind. Maybe that's why they're called Psychics.

But I still need to make a living. Hey, what about horse racing? I could predict what horse will win the next race and put a big bet on it. Or sell my predictions to other bettors. Saratoga is an easy drive from here. And there are OTB places all over around here. I wonder if they would let me sell my predictions? Probably not. And if I was always right, they wouldn't believe I was a witch, they would claim I was cheating, in league with the jockeys or trainers. And that makes me think again about how I find out if I can predict. I don't have the money to make bets on 50 or 100 races, to see how I do. Unless, of course, I win every race. But I don't know if I can do that. Maybe until I find out, I better not start making a living that way.

Or I could go to the casino and use my powers there. Not on the slots. They're too fast and too noisy. But maybe at the craps tables, or the blackjack tables. I bet I could clean up at the casino. Though I heard they ban people who win too much. They say those people must be cheating. Is using your witchy powers cheating? But if the casino is going to watch me and sooner or later ban me, then I'm not trying it.

I've thought about these things for several days. Finally, I've realized that I really am not a witch (sorry, Grandma Mercy). And I can't make a living with my "witchy" powers.

I also knew that I still needed to make a living. I've looked at some more help wanted ads but I've gotten nowhere. I know I don't want to work in a fast-food place, and not in a hotel making beds. Waiting tables sounds awful: on my feet all the time, putting up with crabby customers, having to suck up to everybody in order to get good tips! I can't work in a nursing home or any health care facility, because I don't have any training for it. I've seen some more ads for help in animal shelters. Maybe I ought to think about that a little bit. I do like animals, especially dogs. I think I'll try for it.

Today is the first anniversary of my high school graduation. I still work at an animal shelter, and like it. But I only work there part time now. The rest of the time I take classes and study. I'm enrolled in the veterinary college. First, I'll get an associate degree and become an Animal Health Technician. I like that, because I can keep working at the animal shelter that I like so much, and in a new position with more responsibility than my first job there. And if I want to go on further to get a DVM eventually, I'll be in a good starting place. Overall, I think I'm doing better now than I would as a working witch.

CREATIVE ELDERS

CHAPTER TWO

Poetry

TREE OF LIFE: Polly Ginsberg

Ronnie Uss, "Creative Connections,"
tile mosaic, Roarke Center, Troy, NY

SECTION 1

Rhymes

PROGRESS?

Stephanie Bollam

Fifty ways to meet and greet:

Blogs and Facebook,

Twitter, Tweet.

Gone the handshakes;

Gone the smiles;

Gone the phones,

     with clicks and dials.

Now, we've smart ones,

     sleek and lean,

User friendly,

     tap the screen.

Text a message;

Join the "cloud";

Techno nerds have

     done us proud!

CHOOSING THREAD

Frances H. Berg

I needed white, but what a fright.
I should have seen that this is green.
It will not do. Not even blue
Would be just right. I still need white.
Could I instead perhaps use red?
Or even pink? What do you think?
I think I might still find some white.

USING THREAD

Frances H. Berg

If I could see the needle's eye,
I'd put this thread right through it.
Or so I think until I try,
And somehow I can't do it.
Now my frustration's getting high,
So maybe I could glue it.
It's at the other end, oh my,
Now there, it's done. I knew it.

NOW

Frances H. Berg

Now is the before, for lack
Ten minutes hence you might want back.
A careless word, attention lapse.
A broken trust, or bone, perhaps.
Now is the before. Take care.
Pay attention. Be aware.

HEALTH

Frances H. Berg

A sneeze and a sniffle and a raspiness of throat
Presage loss of health of which you were about to gloat.
Your head starts pounding and your tongue has got a coat.
The aches in your muscles make you feel like stewed compote.
So head for your easy chair, don't let it get your goat.
Take plenty of fluids till you feel about to float.
An aspirin can help, if you believe the doctor's quote.
I know from experience, so this is what I wrote.

KATYDID

Frances H. Berg

A katydid with note so shrill
Sat upon my window sill
Chirped away his "dids" and didn'ts
Till I shooed him off, good riddance.

AND THAT'S WHY

(for my granddaughter)
Frances H. Berg

How did the popcorn get under
    the bed?
Somebody probably didn't
    want bread.
Made a nice bowlful of
    popcorn instead,
Tripped on a shoelace and
    bumped his poor head,
Scattering popcorn, then
    hastily fled,
And that's why the popcorn
    is under the bed.

ON AGING

Vince Powers

My water in the morn is now a tool
For taking lots of pills, which feels so cruel.
I see my skin, as smooth as silk of yore,
Is now some wrinkly stuff that I deplore.
My legs that used to let me run and hike
Are now two weak old things that I don't like.
My eyes can't see to read except large print;
To watch TV I really have to squint.

My body tells me I am old.
But my soul is saying age is gold.
Now I'm more content with life,
Accepting all without due strife.
My problems are not now my care;
Of all my gifts I'm more aware.

SECTION 2

Haiku—
Images of Nature

*The rhythm, brevity and descriptive
power of Haiku appealed to five of us.*

Summer

SUMMER

Vince Powers

It is very hot
And with high humidity –
I think of snowfalls.

MIDSUMMER

Jane Comerford, CSJ

People-faced pansies
Now bow to noble roses,
And life continues.

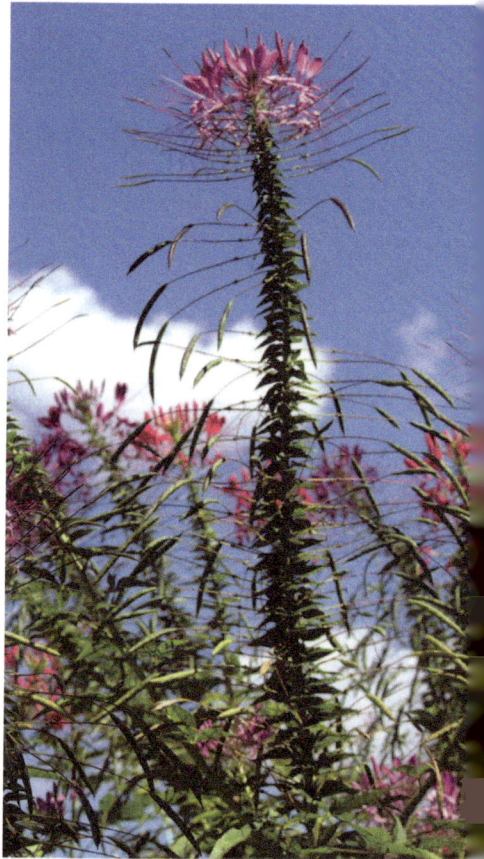

Ted Zborowski, Wildflowers

GARDENS

Vince Powers

Beautiful flowers
Brighten my eyes and my soul.
Thank you for them, God.

UNTITLED

Mary Ann Lettau

In the wild June wind
The new leaves wave and flutter.
Dance now. Fall will come.

INSECT SIGHTING

Ann M. Krupski

A praying mantis
Such a surprising sighting
Rare summer moment

MEDITATION

Ann M. Krupski

Gaze at a flower
Delight in magnificence
Enter timeless space

DEW

Ann M. Krupski

Take time with dewdrops
Reflection miniatures
Beauty is calling

Fall

SKY

Ann M. Krupski

See what sky reveals
Colors speak decisively
As if clouds listen

UNTITLED

Mary Ann Lettau

A growl of thunder,
A zig-zagging light; black clouds
Then pour out their hearts.

CYCLE

Ronnie Uss

Earth pulls darkness down
We grow quiet. We sleep.
Sunlight starts the day.

A RAINY DAY

Vince Powers

The rain is heavy,
And it makes me feel depressed –
Remember the sun!

Winter

TREES

Ronnie Uss

Tall trees guard the earth
Wooden sentinels keep watch
Spring is coming soon

Katelyn Dwyer, Willow Tree Winter, part of the Shaker Pointe
campus across the road.

UNTITLED

Mary Ann Lettau

1   Early winter broods
　　In brown and grey; no snow yet
　　To cover sadness.

2   The winter will end.
　　They all do. Spring is foretold
　　In the Book of Birds.

3   Patches of grey snow
　　And ice-covered rotted leaves.
　　The forest hides hope.

4   Each snowflake unique-
　　"No two alike," until they
　　Splat on the windshield.

5   Winds with bated breath
　　Await the snow. Nothing stirs.
　　Hush. The flakes descend.

Spring

LEAVES

Ann M. Krupski

Touch a leaf and learn
New leaves are always tender
Weather changes them

UNTITLED

Mary Ann Lettau

1   The gray-green curtain
    Of Spanish moss is swaying,
    Blown by ghostly winds.

2   Snow on daffodils.
    Rain today. Sun tomorrow.
    Indecisive Spring.

3   Daffodils, tulips,
    Forsythia, hyacinths—
    At long last—color.

WHOOSH!

Ronnie Uss

Birds feed on the ground
Large shadow is overhead
Suddenly, no birds.

PARTNERS

Ronnie Uss

Geese fly two by two
Their life bond made visible
Sharing gosling care.

ILLUSION

Ronnie Uss

Gold flowers on trees
Instantly, they all take flight
Bright spots in the sky

SPRING

Vince Powers

The bees are buzzing,
The robins are singing loud.
New life emerges.

Kateln Dwyer, Willow Tree Spring, part of the Shaker Pointe campus across the road.

SECTION 3

Musings

HAIKU

Ann M. Krupski

Haiku poetry
Less is more explains itself
Haiku amazement

REALITY

Ronnie Uss

It is always now
There is no past, no future.
Only the present

BEING HEARD

Ronnie Uss

Talk to the closet
It hangs on your ev'ry word
Stores all your stories

WARM WELCOME

Ann M. Krupski

Warmth in a welcome

Genuine gestures of love

Robust feast for all

INSPIRATION

Ann M. Krupski

Inspired by love

Absorbed in moments of light

All action transformed

TIME

Ann M. Krupski

Time can pass slowly

Then, again, not always so

Time's deceptions rule

BEING

Ann M. Krupski

Sitting, just looking
Not really doing a thing
Effortless being

INSOMNIA

Ann M. Krupski

Body wide awake
Restlessness without rivals
Insomnia reigns

KINDNESS

Ann M. Krupski

When kindness guides days
Doing good prompts all actions
Hearts fill completely

MY LOVE

Vince Powers

I miss her daily
Her spirit enlivened me–
Life is dimmer now

MISSING

Ann M. Krupski

Time spent, completed
Heart's gentle remembering
Missing's marathon

SECTION 4

Free Verse

THE TUFTED TITMOUSE

Lisa Cirillo, CSJ

Yesterday,
On the bare branch
Outside my window,
I saw a Tufted Titmouse.
She was sweet and saucy
As she poised there, and my heart
Was touched by her.

Today,
I looked for her once more.
I watched quietly and patiently.
I heard her chirp nearby;
Then glimpsed her
In the higher branches,
But she did not come
To my bare branch
Again.

Today,

I watched for God,

Looking in the same spot

I saw him yesterday.

And yet, I know,

That, like the Tufted Titmouse,

He may not come again

To that same branch

Where he was yesterday,

Or even with

The same feathers on.

I know

That I may hear him,

Or catch a glimpse,

But must wait and watch

With patience

For him to come and sit nearby

Again.

SEQUENCE

Mary Ann Lettau

Greens of summer,
All hues and tints:
  moss, fern, sage, dill,
  arugula,
  peas, zucchini,
  clover, lettuce,
   corn stalks.

Bright greens in sunny fields,
Black greens in shrouded woods.

Leaves of summer,
All shapes and sizes:
  spiky new grass,
  curvy maples,
  delicate fronds,
  pointy-edged oaks,
   grape vines.

Then,
Autumn foliage
Parades in Joseph's coat:
  neon yellow,
  hot-pepper orange,
  rich bronze, olive,
  mahogany,
   sharp red.

The leaves hang loosely;
sharp winds toss the colors
like confetti.

The colored chips drift to earth,
turning brown under the snow,
to feed Spring growth and
Summer greens.

Ted Zborowski, Seasons

WIND'S LATE AUTUMN GIFT

Ann M. Krupski

How wind plays!
Taking off,
Tossing,
Juggling dry brown leaves.

Like a percussion soloist
striking crisp, staccato sounds
as leaves skitter on cement.

Or a harpist
with invisible hands
creating gentle, rustling arpeggios.

Caught by the sheer delight of such sounds,
wrapped in a breath-taking moment,
I pause.

Wind's unexpected gift.

AN OCTOBER WALK

Ann M. Krupski

On a mild October afternoon,

when the air was fresh,

not quite crisp yet,

two elders

       went for a walk.

Their canes provided security

       for each new step.

An unheard conversation

       revealed a warm bond.

Their faces

       a comfortable intimacy.

This gentle picture

       revealed strength

       greater than canes.

A tender moment

       caught me by surprise.

THE WEEPING BEECH TREE

Janet Troidle

Layer upon layer of gnarled wonder
Tree is dressed like a coifed mushroom
Its girth swollen wide
With four centuries of living and dying.
Some bark is smooth, like a rose petal's skin
Most is leathery grey, like an elephant's trunk.

Grounded in timelessness
Its arms can no longer carry the load
So, they hang, heavily laden
With small oval forest-green leaves
Huddled thickly along its arteries and veins.

The winds of time propel them
Into an ever-constant swirling, motion....
Dangling myriads of tendril
That shade and cool my heart.

Umbrella-like, tree's top
Zipped the sky closed
With its years of growth,
Except for one strong branch
That wormed its way through the fray
To become tree's crooked hat with bird.

No longer forest-green,
But gray-brown and bald, that branch
Voiced strength, perseverance, and faith,
Unfettered by the most furious
Of life's storms.

With feathered touch, I tenderly ran my fingers
Along its smooth trunk
Caressing unmatched beauty.
It exuded all of life's virtue.
My mother, the weeping beech!

SNOWBIRD

Mary Ann Lettau

Hello to Florida!

Butterfly beats
brighten the gray
   of Northern moods.

Baseball and beer
bring cheers and boos—
   don't block my view!

Bustling breezes
blow over Bays:
   Lemon and Tampa.

Beautiful birds
brag with gusto
   In Southern accents.

Bowers of blooms
bless us—just say
  bougainvillea.

April arrives—sad goodbye, to
  mullet, herons,
  dolphins, gators
  lizards, osprey
   manatees.

And to
  strawberries,
  lemon trees,
  cacti, palms,
   and Spanish moss.

SNOW IS BEAUTIFUL,

Mary Ann Lettau

…when
it outlines, in white, the roof,
  eaves, and sills of the red barn;
it clings to angled branches,
  and sparkles on crusty ice.
it's blinding in the cold sun-
  don't squint! Find your sunglasses;
roads, paths, driveways, stairs-hidden;
  we are closed in- time for soup!
…when
leafless trees cast black shadows
  onto smooth hillocks and drifts;
lazy, large flakes float and dance,
  and fall to cover brown earth;
it shapes the hills and valleys
  against the winter blue sky;
it flies horizontally!;
  (wondrous, but your eyes will sting);
tracks— deer, skis, speeding sleds-are
  deeply carved into whiteness.

SNOW IS NOT BEAUTIFUL

Mary Ann Lettau

…when
it's mixed with sleet;
it blackens into ugly slush;
it hides black ice;

…when
it gets into your boots;
it's April…

MOTHER MOON

By Janet Troidle

I did not want to miss this moment
As the round "host" of evening's sky made its slow descent
They called it "The Full Blue Moon"

Stark blue-white against a black night
It answered horizon's call in slow motion

I'm watching, I'm loving…
This magnificent moon is my mother

She touches my soul
In ways I could not have imagined
99 years of rising and setting
…so very weeping tired

Soon, soon she too will descend
And then, then
She will rise again
A vibrant morning glory!

SECTION 5

Fun with Limericks

During the winter of 2022, Shaker Pointe community residents had fun with limericks. The challenge was the rhyme scheme-getting that final line to rhyme with the first two lines.

Corned beef and cabbage make Paddy's mouth drool.

Jacques loves his quiche – he's so very cool!

Who's food is best…

When put to the test???

Giuseppe will always choose pasta fazoole.

By Jean Padula

It's morning and high time to wake her.

So call her or nudge her or Shaker.

And here is the Pointe

There's no nicer joint

For friendship and fun you could take her.

By Frances H. Berg

There once was a young lass named Molly

Who 'twas loved by the lads; by golly!

But the lads were so shy

They couldn't look her in the eye,

So she went home alone on the trolley.

By Carole Egan

A vain man who lives in Doane Brook
Thinks he ought to get more than one look.
    Sam, you're Irish I know,
    But by gosh, even so
You're not handsome, so don't be a schnook.

By Vince Powers

An old guy who moved to the Pointe
Discovered his knee out of joint
    He walked and he talked
    He never would have balked
'Cause the welcome did not disappoint.

By Richard Shirey

A young Irish guest named O'Toole
Was invited to splash in the pool
    "With its temp eighty-three
    It's for sure," said he,
"I'd rather be hot than be cool!

By Eileen Shirey

Shaker Pointe has seniors galore.

They're good and we wish there were more.

When all's said and done,

They have lots of fun;

We love the Shaker Pointe corps.

By Vince Powers

CHAPTER THREE

Non-Fiction

TREE OF LIFE: Charla Whimple, CSJ

MY FATHER

Barbara Donnaruma

I remember my father as a tall fair-haired man with piercing blue eyes. He was a quiet man who talked only to teach me.

He taught me how to wash a dish. I remember him whenever I load the dishwasher.

He taught me to drive on a busy highway where new drivers are no longer allowed to learn to drive. When I exited the off ramp in front of a fast-moving truck, he quietly said, "Just step on the gas."

Most of all he said about whatever I was doing, "Slow down, little girl, slow down."

He called me little girl because I had two sisters. He would call one name, then another. Eventually he gave up and just said little girl.

As he aged, he developed a disease which kept him from swallowing very well and caused his eyelids to droop. He tried to tell stories. I had a hard time listening and because I would never do two things when I could do three, I never heard what happened to Ed Delaney at the gas company.

I miss my father. But something happened a few years ago. While on vacation with my fair-haired grandson, I was rushing around the hotel room, gathering things to meet our tour group. I heard a voice from the other side of the room, "Slow down, Grandma. Slow down."

THE ROSE'S VOICE

Pat Musick Carr

A single rose, significantly white poised in a glass vase awaiting flight.

I lay on a rough, scratchy blanket stretched upon the mountain meadow. It was dark, impenetrably dark. Looking west I saw a small ball of light arcing the Finger Lakes skies. Its trajectory, a line curving eastward, then lost to sight.

I wondered, "Who are those guys up there and what are they like?" Six years later I married one of them.

I call them "ordained occasions" — one of those things just meant to happen—not luck, accident, or predestination— just meant to occur and become part of the memory.

For forty-two years I gave Jerry Carr a single white rose on November 16th in celebration of the launch of Skylab IV, the 84-day mission of the United States' first space station.

The rose was a remembrance of the rookie Commander's indescribable journey. The flower's perky, white bulbous shape and long, streaming stem symbolize that breathless moment before liftoff and the thrusting penetration of the heavens. Its slow-blooming movement is a metaphor for the spinoffs with which space enriches our planet. The gradually

fading aroma reminds us of the fragile nature of existence and exhorts us to value each day.

Launched in a flurry of blinding light, its trajectory, the void...out of sight.

THE MOON'S BUTTERFLY

Eileen Shirey

Who would ever think that a butterfly could form an indelible impression on one's mind? Or even that over the course of years, a total of four butterflies would succeed in doing so? This story is actually the combination of four different butterfly stories which I have come to regard as the butterfly-connection.

The first butterfly story was relayed by a woman I visited as a Hospice chaplain. Joan was the primary care giver for her dying grandmother. But Joan's primary grief was still centered on the loss of her beautiful sixteen-year-old daughter Amy in an auto accident on prom night of the previous spring. Joan described her months-long, devastating struggle to hang onto her sanity. She then proclaimed that a very strange event helped enormously to put her on the path of healing.

In the throes of grief, all Joan could think about was wanting to be with Amy for even one more minute and in that time to know that Amy was OK. Joan's bereavement group, named Emerging Butterflies, encouraged her to be open to that possibility – somehow, somewhere. Then, on Christmas Eve, a particularly bitter cold Christmas Eve, Joan bundled up to attend midnight mass. She opened the door to her front porch, flipped on the porch light and what did she see but a single monarch butterfly circling the light. Enfolded by a deep sense of peace, Joan stood transfixed for several moments. When she eventually continued out the door, the butterfly flew out with her and vanished into the night. In church that evening, Joan could think of nothing but that butterfly and the deep peace that remained with her. Joan was certain that for Christmas, she had been granted her deepest wish to be with Amy.

A few weeks after hearing this remarkable story, I was informed by Hospice that as a result of an institutional reorganization, my part-time position no longer existed. I was no longer to be a Hospice chaplain. I interpreted this turn of events as personal failure and entered into my own bout of deep grief. Like Joan I struggled to get out of bed each morning and put one foot in front of the other. One Saturday my husband encouraged me to join him in a game of golf – mainly to get me out into the sunshine.

Ted Zborowski, Monarch

So, following a decent drive, there I was on the fairway walking toward my ball – and a monarch butterfly was circling the ball. Immediately thinking of Joan's story, I played along with this coincidence. Let's see… Who would visit me on the golf course? Obviously, this had to be my Dad, the guy who taught me to play. Taking this idea even further I said to the butterfly, "Well,

Dad, what did you think of my drive? Do you think my swing has improved any?"

Having amused myself for that moment, I proceeded onward with the game and was pleased to arrive on the green in a total of five really decent shots. And there, about twenty long feet from the hole lay my golf ball – once again circled by a butterfly - the butterfly? It continued to circle even as I addressed the putt. Trying to send it away, I waved my putter over the ball, but the persistent butterfly did not give an inch. Not wanting to hit it with the putter, I rather impatiently shooed the butterfly aside and quickly took my shot without having sized up the putt at all. To my amazement, the ball moved along the twenty-foot path directly toward the pin and plunked into the cup. At this point, my knees began to quiver, and quite overwhelmed, I whispered, "Thanks, Dad!"

Now fast-forward twenty years. My Mom had been living an active life as a widow until 2008. On the eve of her 90th birthday party, she slumped to the floor with a broken hip. Then for an additional six years she lived in an adult home where, after rehabilitation, she continued to enjoy life. She especially appreciated the company of the other residents and the staff-organized activities, one of which was the late summer project of hatching butterflies from cocoons. This venture concluded with a special party where the butterflies were released into their intended places in nature.

However, by the summer of 2014, my 96-year-old mother Kathy was diagnosed with vascular blockage in her legs which could not be treated by the preferred method of catheterization. Thus, Mom was given a choice between two extreme surgeries, neither of which was she likely to survive. She vehemently rejected the surgery route and so, by default, Mom could only wait for the gangrene in her toes to become septic – and snuff out her life. Thank heavens, Mom was welcomed back to the adult home where she did her best to carry on as much as normal. Her friends were not informed of Mom's condition, but they later told me that each night she cried and they cried along with her. In her last days Mom suffered great pain. I also cried long and hard by her side.

The day of the butterfly-release found Mom lying in a coma in Hospice. Back at the Adult home that afternoon, there had been a long delay of the main event because the reporter from the local newspaper did not arrive to photograph the event and publish the results for the usual follow-up public relations article. Eventually it was decided to go ahead with the butterfly-release in which each resident's name was given to a freed butterfly. At the end, it was decided that a butterfly should be released in Kathy's name. And when one was, the butterfly flew directly up to Kathy's second-floor window sill where it rested for a long time.

At this point, you may have counted three butterfly stories. The last butterfly story happened a week later when the newspaper reporter came to record a second release-party arranged for the sake of the PR article. This party was held about three days after Kathy's funeral. Again, the butterflies were released in the name of each resident in attendance. Again, the last butterfly was dedicated to Kathy – and again that butterfly flew up and rested on Mom's windowsill.

But how does the butterfly-connection fit into my thoughts about life after death? Perhaps the Buddha gives a good concept for trying to put words to any statement about Ultimate Reality which all religious traditions agree is unknowable. He says that all words that try to name or describe The Unknowable (Christians substitute "God") are fingers pointing to the moon. The fingers point to the moon, but they are not the moon. So, for me, the Amy-Dad-Mom-butterflies are fingers pointing to the Moon.

And what are they trying to say about the Moon? If I were to name the Moon's butterfly, I would call her Undying Love.

A HUMMINGBIRD IN MY HAND

Ann M. Krupski

Hummingbirds amaze me. In New York State, ruby-throated ones are the most common. They usually arrive in early May, leaving in early September, around Labor Day. Quite a short stay.

Many years ago, our house was prepared for these amazing birds. A hanging feeder on the back deck; a fully flowering bright red and purple fuchsia outside the guest room window; another hanging feeder outside the windows on the front side of the house. The house was definitely ready and became a haven for many hummingbirds.

One beautiful, clear blue sky, sunny June morning, I looked out the glass sliding door facing the back deck. I immediately spotted our six-month-old, long-haired tortoiseshell cat. Pumpkin was on the ground with something in her mouth. Although no one was home, I loudly exclaimed with great distress: "THAT'S A HUMMINGBIRD!"

Proceeding with great care, I moved slowly towards my favorite new cat. I spoke to her gently and softly. She did not move away. It was probably the first time she had caught a flying bird. I continued to move cautiously, stopped, and slowly bent down to get closer to her.

Somehow, I really don't know how, I was able to get the hummingbird out of her mouth. The bird was noticeably stunned but was not bleeding anywhere that I could see.

This little bird, about two inches long, fit in the palm of my left hand. I slid the heavy glass door open with my right hand making sure that Pumpkin did not follow me inside. Then I slid the door closed.

Once inside the living area, I cupped my right hand over the left. The hummingbird did not move but felt warm in my hand. I recalled what friends of mine, who owned a bird store, had told me about what to do when a bird was in shock after hitting a window.

'Put the bird in a small, brown paper lunch bag. Crimp

the edges loosely. Let the bird be. If not severely injured,

the bird will recover in the warmth and dark. Then it will fly

out after about twenty minutes or so.'

Because there were many large windows in the house, I had the opportunity to put these steps into use numerous times. Never with a hummingbird.

Unable to access a lunch bag, I continued to keep my curved right hand over the left. The space between my hands must have been cave-like, warm, and dark. It felt like I was holding everything and nothing simultaneously. After all, these precious little beings, when full grown, weigh about 0.12 of an ounce – less than the weight of a nickel.

While holding this absolutely still hummingbird, I paced and prayed. During that forty-minute period, I reflected. "This little being had flown alone, hundreds of miles to get here to our neighborhood. The challenges of its flight were untold." One inexperienced kitten had stopped it mid-air.

As I continued to pace, there was no movement from the bird. It felt warm; and I felt peaceful. At one point, after many minutes, I felt an ever so tiny scratch in my palm. It was like someone taking a sharp pin and moving it lightly a fraction of an inch.

Encouraged, I opened that heavy glass sliding door and stepped onto the deck. I stood in the warmth of the sun, lifted up my right hand and unfurled my left one. The bird did not move. I quickly recreated its cave with my hands and went back inside the house. I resumed my pacing but with a sense of hope. Within minutes, I felt a more significant scratching on my left palm.

Out I went again and repeated all of my previous movements. When my hand was open to the sunshine, the hummingbird was alert and still for a moment. Then it lifted off my open hand. I saw its ruby throat and knew it was a male.

As he flew up very high in the direction of the trees, I called up to him,

"STAY AWAY FROM CATS!"

John R. Pattison, Rhizobium

THE PLANT BIOLOGY OF COVER CROPPING

John R. Pattison

"Rhizobium is a Bacterium" *...or so says Inge Eley, my 'plant biology coach' here where I live in Upstate New York.*

We were talking about plants, and the value of cover cropping. And I had asked a question knowing I'd get a set-you-back-on-your-heels kind of answer.

My question to Inge was, "How do certain plant species set nitrogen in the soil?" I've heard about this throughout my years of gardening, living in a farming community in Rensselaer County. She told me that the roots of plants of the legume family, for example, develop nodules in which Rhizobium lives. This is the stuff that absorbs air's most plentiful component, nitrogen.

So, what is there about good garden soil that we "pop-in-the-car, toss-in-the-trash" beings need to know for planetary survival? And how can Rhizobium be of any use to us in this epic struggle???

She continued to explain that Rhizobium is a beneficial bacterium. Roots of legume species left in the ground decompose leaving nitrogen for the next crop to feast upon. She further explained that nothing happens with the collected nitrogen until bacteria chemically transform it into useable nitrogen, just what new plants need. It's like baseball: short stop scoops up the ball, but no points scored till the ball gets to the second baseman, who steams it over to the first baseman, each with his respective foot on the base. It's nature's high-caliber teamwork; ruthless efficiency - common in nature, rare in baseball.

So, I wonder, again looking at Inge, if the roots attract nitrogen from the air, and the roots are underground, where does the air come from? The answer says a lot about the difference between good garden soil and just plain old dirt.

It's called diversity. Clay is hard and dense. Maybe good for roads and tennis courts, not for gardens. But add ingredients like peat moss, animal manure and composted vegetation and clay becomes lighter, looser, more friendly for air and water. This time good for gardens, not for roads or tennis courts.

Good soil needs to be maintained. Centuries of gardeners/ farmers have successfully practiced replacing soil nutrients that their crops have used up. When your plants dry up at seasons end, sow a cover crop and get out of the way. Your hard-working earthworms and bees will rejoice at the new diversity in the neighborhood, and your soil will be eager to greet your next season's plant decisions.

"Rhizobium!" – Cute name for something so basic to survival on the planet!

A LESSON FROM THE DANDELION

Barbara Donnaruma

My sister would never kill a plant, not knowingly, not willingly.

However, she lived in a suburban area that valued the green, lush, weed-free front lawn. So one day in early summer, she ventured out into her yard armed with a sharp garden knife and a basket.

On her hands and knees, she proceeded to dig the dandelions out of the grass. After an hour or so of hard labor, she heard her name called from the street, "Mrs. Forrest, Mrs. Forrest."

She looked up and saw her neighbor's three little girls in their summer play clothes.

Each was holding a beautiful, fully blossomed dandelion puffball.

In unison, they each took a deep breath and blew.

Pat Musick Carr, "Good morning world!"

LADYBUG AND ROCKY

Pat Musick Carr

Each morning at dawning I go to their kennel
Pure love emerging, never judgmental,
Wishing only to give every measure
of themselves...unconditional treasure.

I open the chain-link gate and two sleepy brown and white speckled bundles shake their way to my side. Together we walk to the edge of the 200-foot cliff that defines our valley below. Soft round fields, and crisply cascading river pay homage to the pale pink sky. My hands rest on the velvet-eared heads and I deeply inhale the morning breeze. Quiet awaits the dawn's imminent explosion.

It is a morning ritual, and the dogs know every second of it. They do not move, and together we signal silent delight. I lift my arms to the warming sky and say, "Good morning world," a sign our morning ritual is ended, and they are free to explore their valley. I watch as the spotted camouflage disappears into the woods, searching for squirrels and bunnies.

A daily occasion over the years
births memories of joy, my eyes fill with tears.

TWINKLE TOES COMES TODAY

Ann M. Krupski

As an elementary school music educator, I taught grades Kindergarten through eighth in the 1960s and 1970s. My goal was to help young people develop concepts of melody, harmony, rhythm, and form. That goal was accomplished through singing, moving, playing rhythm instruments and autoharp and by guided listening to portions of select orchestral works. In a half hour period, we usually did three different activities.

When I learned about programs that worked with nursery school children, I observed a former student teach classes of three and four-year-olds. Although I was retired from teaching classroom music, I was inspired. As soon as I could, I signed up for certification training.

The following memories have been significant ones.

Once certified, I knew I needed to get an assistant. Twinkle Toes got the job. She is a finger puppet mouse. Her color is light gray with pink feet and big pink inner ears. Her tail is almost as long as her five-inch body. Two fingers fit into her extended legs.

Twinkle Toes went with me to the varied groups I taught. In a thirty-minute class, we did between eight and ten activities – all focused-on music learning. Young children love music, are receptive to its many moods, and learn quickly – even words and concepts like accelerando and crescendo. Twinkle

Toes often whispered instructions in my ear.

If you have ever been in a setting with a group of youngsters, you know the importance attached to being the leader of a line of classmates. One morning, as the four-year-olds lined up after our class, I saw that one girl was crying. There was a mix-up about who the line leader was. When I asked her if she would like to carry Twinkle Toes back to the classroom, the crying stopped immediately. She held that little mouse as if it were a trophy she had just won.

Like each of us, young children appreciate being called by name. As we began each class, Twinkle Toes and I sang a greeting to each child. Classroom teachers had helped with name tags.

At the end of one class, we stood up from our places in the circle on the floor. I bent down to say something to one of the boys. He quickly covered his name tag. Luckily, I had just seen his name and was able to call him Ben. He was quick to test me, and I was successful that time.

Later in the month, I had recognized Ben in a parking lot by a local pharmacy. As soon as he noticed me, he happily called: "So how's the mouse?" He hadn't called me by name, but he certainly knew who I was. More important, he knew Twinkle Toes.

One summer, I volunteered at a local retreat center. Families spent weeks at a time there. The three and four-year-olds were provided with classes. Each Wednesday at 10 AM I did the music class. Twinkle Toes was always with me. Even parents participated as enthusiastically as the children.

One week a parent shared the following story. A young girl from the class was talking with her Mom. She said: "Mommy, what day is it?" The Mom responded: "It's Wednesday." The girl brightened and said "Oh good! Twinkle Toes comes today."

I'm retired now. Twinkle Toes sits by my side, wondering if the children will come today.

ONE EASTER MORNING

Catherine A. Kruegler, C.S.J.

It was a bright and breezy Easter Sunday morning in South Texas.

Sr. Cathy and Sr. Bridget were relaxing after a late-night vigil and having breakfast in the small kitchen in the Primera Colonia, when the phone rang and broke the celebratory morning.

It was Sr. Jean calling from the Congregation House in St. Louis with a request for a big favor! She began to tell the story of a woman named, Sylvia, a mother from Guatemala, who had somehow found her way from Guatemala City to the United States and then to St. Louis. On that morning, she was living in Sanctuary with the Sisters. She had been forced to leave her children behind with their grandmother, after their father, a catechist, and a community leader had been killed.

But now Sylvia learned that the military were following the children home from school and asking questions about their mother and uncle and his family. It was decided that the uncle and Sylvia's two children should leave Guatemala quickly and even now were about to come into the Rio Grande Valley on Easter Sunday!

So, the big favor was this: Would we go to the Western Union Office in Brownsville to receive some money to be wired to us. We then needed to meet the uncle, Guillermo, on a side street near Casa Oscar Romero, give him the money so he could pay the "coyote," the human kind, who brought the group from Guatemala into the U.S. Once Guillermo gave the coyote the money, he would get the children back. "But ... but ... [I protested on the phone] what if he gives him the money and this coyote wants more?" It was a chance we had to take.

The coyote demanded a certain amount per person and that is what we were able to raise to give him. The second part of the favor was to bring the uncle to Casa Oscar Romero and get him settled there. They thought it would be safer for the children if they stayed at separate places.

We were asked to take care of the children and to get them on a flight to St. Louis. I heard myself say "well yes, of course!" The implications of all that began to sink in, only on the way to Brownsville in the car. Back then transporting or giving shelter to refugees was illegal and held a penalty of jail if caught.

Well, the exchange with the coyote went smoothly enough. He was happy with the couple of thousand dollars we gave him, and we were on our way. The three had walked through Guatemala and Mexico, hiding from soldiers or dangerous situations, surviving on next to nothing with only the clothes on their backs.

The children: Cory, age 7 and Said, age 5, had sneakers on that were several sizes larger than their little feet and caked with the dirt from the desert. The laces were wrapped around legs and ankles to keep them on. At Casa Romero, when he began to feel safe, Guillermo started to recount the story of when they were about to cross the Rio Grande River. "EI Migro," as they called immigration officials, were nearby. They almost saw Guillermo who was carrying Said, giving him a piggy-back ride. When Guillermo saw the Border Patrol, he ducked down deep in the water, with the child on his back.

Said thought his uncle was playing horsey and began to yell and splash around. They were very afraid Border Patrol had seen them, but thank goodness, they had not! Phew! We got Guillermo settled. With Sr. Julianna at the helm at Casa, and her wonderful kindness, we knew he was in good hands. Then we got on the road with the children for the 40-minute ride to Primera.

First things first. We shared what was to be our Easter meal of ham and potatoes and vegetables – not a Guatemalan menu, but the children were so hungry the plates were wiped clean. Next, a shower and to bed in our T-shirts. I put them both to sleep in my twin bed. I remember standing in the doorway a long time after they fell asleep. They looked like two little angels.

Bridget and I were exhausted from the stress and activity of the day, but I could only imagine all that these little ones had been through. They looked so cute with their dark hair, and big brown eyes now closed in sleep. Then I called St Louis to say: "Mission Accomplished."

The next morning, Sr. Bridget took care of the children, and I went down the road a mile or so to the Airport to get tickets for three to Dallas. I arranged with the airline to care for the children from Dallas to St. Louis. I would have given anything to see their reunion in St. Louis with their mother, but it would be costly for the extra adult ticket and legally dangerous.

After all the travel arrangements were made, we could have a bit of fun. I brought the children to Sears in the nearby mall. After all these years, I still can see the wide-eyed expression of wonder on their faces when they saw the huge American department store. "O Dios Mio," Cory uttered, as they looked at all the clothes and toys!

We picked out ordinary play clothes, something American children might wear to visit relatives the day after Easter. Cory liked a sky-blue play suit and white T shirt. It was khaki slacks and a pastel plaid shirt for Said. Then to find some new sneakers that fit, so we could pitch the others. After all the trying on and looking around we made time and had enough resources for some jellybeans and a stuffed animal for each.

Luckily, I had been in the Airport many times and had a good feel for what the under-cover INS folks looked for in picking up the undocumented. I still felt very nervous about getting the children from "The Valley" to Dallas, but I couldn't show it and I needed to keep the kids very calm. After all, we were just on an Easter visit.

Once in Dallas we got some lunch and got to the children's gate for departure. I had only known Cory and Said for three days but it felt like a lifetime. I stood and watched as the stewardess helped them both with the early pre-boarding. I was pretty sure the airlines would get them to their Mom safely, but as I stood and watched them go through the door to the ramp the tears rolled down my face. What a saga in their very young lives and maybe I would never see them again? I knew it was an Easter I would never forget. New Life for all of us!

POST SCRIPT:

I had gotten word of course, from Sr. Jean that the children had arrived in St. Louis safe and sound and united with their mother. I thought that was the end: they would go on with their lives and I with my ministry. Guillermo, on the other hand, who was staying at Casa Romero, was out walking around the block and had been picked up by Border Patrol and was in detention. From St. Louis, the Sisters were able to get him legal help. He filled out his Asylum Papers, so was quickly able to travel to Sylvia and the children in St. Louis. His own wife and children were still in Guatemala City. He hoped one day to bring them to the States to be with him.

Fast forward four years later. Our congregation was having a retreat in St. Louis entitled, "Option for The Poor." I had been home in New York for the summer. I had planned to make this retreat on my way cross country and before going back to my ministry in Texas. The retreat was moving along nicely, and we were told there were going to be some refugees with us in the afternoon who were willing to share their story.

Guillermo came into the room first with his wife Teresa and their children. I couldn't quite comprehend what was happening? Then Sylvia, whom I had not met, Cory and Said were introduced. It was my turn to say, "0 Dios Mio"! I felt myself get out of my seat sobbing and started to hug the children first and then the whole family. Of course then I needed to tell all the Sisters on the retreat why I was such a happy, emotional mess! It was a totally joyous reunion.

Said now age 9 and Cory now 11 had grown so beautifully. Guillermo had been able to bring his wife and children, and I met them for the first time. What I did not know was that they had not been able to receive permanent asylum in the U.S., so had gone north to Canada and had been living there for some time. The children had learned English quickly and well and had grown to be confident, loving, and loved young people.

So, if you get a call some Easter morning, from hundreds of miles away don't be afraid to say "yes." It just might be an adventure you'll never forget!

A STORY UNWRITTEN

Barbara Donnaruma

I began to write a travel mystery. I had a great plot, terrific characters, a gorgeous setting-but few facts.

My fantasy like my art, my cooking, my needlework seemed to hang out there in space, ungrounded, unreal, but beautiful in its own way.

My friend asked how it was going and I complained. Then I told her how I went to my husband's travel diary and tried to ground my story as he had written in the details of our trip to Rome in the Jubilee Year 2000.

To my astonishment what I read led me to believe we had not been on the same trip at all.

We had joked for years that we would retire to a tropical island (Kauai to be exact) where we would own a bookstore carrying only travel books (his side) and books of self-discovery through art, reading, painting and spiritual pursuits (my side). We would call it "For your Inner and Outer Journey".

In Rome, I saw a magnificent old hotel with brick court yards, bell pulls, and high ornate ceilings. Furniture from another era. I remember three older, soft-spoken sisters taking their very first trip abroad. One of them stepped onto the Metro going the wrong way and the tour guide went after her on a rescue mission.

Another woman traveling alone made an unpleasant nuisance of herself complaining loudly especially about men. When my husband asked me to hold a poster he had purchased while he took a quick photo, she declared, "They are all like that. He gets what he wants, and she has to do all the carrying."

A lovely young woman sought our company as the handsome Italian tour guide had his eyes on her and she didn't want to start anything. I noticed she did go off to dinner with him on our last night without protest and without seeking our help in any way.

Another very touching vignette was at the Lido beach on our way to Ostia Antica for lunch at the Café a Mare by the Mediterranean-yes, in January. Seafood, pasta, wine. Spectacular! I sat next to my new, loud, unpleasant friend who told me she didn't feel well. This was her second back-to-back tour. She wanted to relax from her job where she worked as a counselor in a clinic. She regaled me with tales of keeping a bowl of condoms on her desk instead of candy, and loved the horrified expression of some of the teens coming in for their appointments.

Happily, I had a mind-clearing walk on the beach and breathed deeply, exhaling the distressing image of an already troubled teenager experiencing more embarrassment. And I did not sit next to the woman on the next leg of the journey.

The view from St. Peter's roof stunned me with its enormity. This was what the Pope would see from his balcony. The Christmas crèche was still there. At the Vatican, unlike US department stores, Christmas did not end on December 26[th.]

The smell of bread, cheese, pasta, the sound of the lovely little Vespas rumbling on the street, the stylish dress of the Italian ladies. No blue jeans here and even in the year 2000, everyone on a cell phone.

Time flew by in Rome: the interior of St. Peter's; the statues by Bernini everywhere–including St. Teresa in Ecstasy, exhibiting for all the world to see what faith can do for the human soul and body.

I've returned to Rome a few more times with my excellent travel guide, companion, lover, husband, but that first visit in the Jubilee year left its impression on me. Yes, that first time, my coin did land directly into the fountain at Trevi. Perhaps I will go again, maybe not.

My memories though, like my watercolors run together like the paint making ever new combinations, beauty, and experience.

We never did see our young lady friend again. Perhaps it wasn't the guide she was avoiding but the disapproval of other tour members. And the large loud lady left before the tour ended. There were rumors that her ill-health was real. We never knew.

As I said, my husband has a different tale to tell.

Facts in this story were verified by my husband!

CODFISH BREAKFAST

John R. Pattison

Salt cod properly prepared in a cream sauce has been a long -time favorite dish of mine.

As it happens, I like to cook, and have made this cod offering whenever I can find a few folks who also seem to enjoy cod. Believe me, they are few and far between.

Many years ago, we had a summer camp on a hemlock-surrounded lake. We would go there to escape the city heat during July and August. I happened to run across a few of these rare codfish aficionados at camp. Campers were watching the kids at a swimming event where the moms were catching up with each other while the guys were doing the same.

Tom, who also likes to cook, said something about cod as an alternative to all the burgers, steak and chicken that neighboring campers seemed to prefer.

"Yikes!" I almost jumped out of my skin. Can I believe I'm talking to another codfish fan?

It was true! We worked up a serious appetite kicking around the various ways to prepare cod. Don't ask me who won the swimming meet.

Over the course of the summer this conversation expanded to the point where we had identified other campers who also connected with codfish memories. And many who didn't,

SALTED COD
in a wooden box

"Count me out when it comes to salt-cod," they would say.

It's a bit like anchovies: a love/hate kind of thing.

The summer camp season closes like the hatchway on a diving submarine when Labor Day arrives. Kids need to be back in school, so everyone packs up to get back to the real world.

Tom and I conjured up a scheme for a Labor Day Codfish Breakfast. Those of us who would enjoy such an event before parting ways agreed it would start with real salt cod in the wooden box, and who would do what, where and when we would meet. We had the temerity to think a few of us could just gather at my camp about 8:30 to 9:00 on Labor Day Morning, sit around on beach chairs, live ashes in the firepit. Soon we'd be eating creamed cod served on roasted potatoes, sipping strong coffee, and then getting on with the exodus with bikes and canoes strapped to the tops of our cars.

But word got out! All of a sudden everyone wanted codfish.

What really happened is everybody wanted a big sendoff at the end of summer camp season, a twist that really cramped the hopes and dreams of us codfish freaks.

Of course, I rationalized, it's about more than just cod. It's about friends and all that. But it's also about cod! Now the codfish junta is compelled to share space with the yet-to-be-enlightened landlubbers. They'll insist on scrambled eggs with bacon or sausage, toast, not roasted potatoes, Bloody Marys, not coffee. And worst of all, they'll be looking down their noses at my plate thinking, "Yuck!"

We staged the event. It was a big sendoff for weeping campers seeing their Brigadoon world folding before their eyes. The "yet to be enlightened" brought their scrambled eggs, toast, Bloody Marys; and the Codfish crew had their creamed cod from a wooden box with mushroom/red pepper/petit pois added, then ladled onto small roasted potatoes and, of course, all with strong black coffee.

It was not the four or five guys contentedly sitting on lawn chairs, though! There were people all over the camp, noise level at fever pitch from the social intensity of the moment, all in a camp cabin with small capacity for food prep. The codfish had to be prepared the previous evening to make the kitchen available for "the unenlightened" to use the inside stove. Codfish could be warmed outside on the little firepit with a small fold-up wire cooking rack which, we calculated, would support the pot over the fire.

Codfish guys were outside by the fire waiting to dish up. We decided we would offer some of this delicacy to any who would like a taste. As we stood around the firepit, codfish just about ready, someone noticed the legs of the wire rack beginning to sink into the hemlock-covered forest floor, making the rack tilt a bit. The pot began to slide. We lunged to grab the pot but couldn't save it; it fell. Some of the precious cargo spilled out onto the forest floor. OMG! What to do? Codfishers decided, "scoop it back into the pot even though there are a few needles and cones mixed in;" nobody was watching.

In we went with our pot of "Codfish Offering," fingers crossed, hoping for things to turn out okay.

Standing there with plate in hand, one of the women said to me, "This is delicious, especially with the added mushrooms/ red pepper/small peas you guys added. And where did you find these delicious little pine-cone-like things?"

Anxiously tuned-in, close-by, Tom caught the drift and panicked. Damage control was needed! He broke in with, "Oh, no one could ever guess what this guy might throw into a traditional recipe! But you can be sure it will be organic, nutritious, and very tasty."

MEANT TO BE

Harold Qualters

In late August of 1957 I started working in my college kitchen as a freshman. After a few weeks of washing dishes, preparing food, and mastering the art of "hey, get me this and that," the chef approached me with the following famous words all people in charge are born with, "Come on, follow me." He brought me to the baking area of the kitchen where bread was being baked every day. He pointed to a machine I had never seen before, and introduced me to a four-to-five-foot, 50-quart Hobart bread mixer. He assured me, as I am sure he caught my somewhat disbelieving face, "in a couple of weeks you'll know precisely how to mix flour, water, yeast and salt."

Immediately, I was fascinated and deeply curious; I felt a deep source of energy gently overcoming me to learn bread making. It was an automatic knowing. It was a moment of joyful energy. I intuitively knew and understood I must learn to make bread. There was no choice. There was peace in the knowing.

And so, I learned well and made bread for the rest of my under graduate days. After I graduated, I kept all my bread notes and recipes in my pocket-size red covered notebook even though I rarely made bread during my career travels. As I reflect on my past and harvest its gifts, I had no inkling that making bread would eventually alter my career path.

The years passed. I married Jeanne and our beautiful

daughter Kate was born in September 1970. A few more years passed. It was 1975. She was now able to watch television with me and we loved the TV show, "Ding Dong School." During one segment of the show, bread was being made. After the show I was momentarily overcome and began to frantically look for my little red, pocket-size bread-making notebook from the kitchen undergraduate years.

You can only imagine what I went through to find the little red, pocket-size bread-making notebook. Luggage, desk drawers, files, bookshelves, boxes filled with stuff, used and unused…but I found it! And I made bread!! And there was great joy in breaking bread with my loving family accompanied by peace in knowing I could still make bread.

I don't recall making bread after that. Career responsibilities called. Once again, I put the little pocket-size red, bread-making notebook away and relegated it to a box where I thought I could find it, just in case – while vaguely knowing many of our life experiences are just meant to be.

Again, wonderful career responsibilities ensued until the summer of 1978. Teacher friends of mine opened a restaurant on Canada Street in Lake George, called the Delevan. Of course, they asked if I would be interested in working in the kitchen during July and August. I was truly excited for this opportunity. Conversation with Jeanne and Kate resulted in a loving YES, and off I went to work at the Delevan with my little red, pocket-size bread-making notebook full of bread recipes not baked since my college years.

Now I had the opportunity to bake my old bread and dessert

recipes which became part of the Delevan breakfast, lunch, and dinner menus. I also became a line cook for breakfast and lunch. And to bring home the old adage that life experiences are meant to be, learning to be a line cook had the future written all over it. The summer of 1978 was truly inspiring, and little did I know what was slowly evolving into my future. However, my pocket-size bread-making notebook stayed secure in my back pocket.

In early September of 1978, I returned home to Jeanne and Kate. I applied for and was granted a one-year sabbatical from my teaching and coaching responsibilities at Shaker High School, in Latham, NY. I would pursue more graduate studies in psychology.

And of course…of course! Enter our dear friend. Tom, a real-estate broker. He had a proposal for us. He had a restaurant for us to buy. We recovered from "What?" "Are you kidding?" "Are you serious?" Tom reflected and confirmed he was very serious!

Additional conversations ensued. Fear, the impact on our loving daughter Kate, emotional confusion, career changes, financial challenges and a whole lot of what ifs followed us everywhere. One late morning, Jeanne turned toward me and said the magic words, "Let's do this!"

In late October of 1978, we purchased the small restaurant/coffee shop in Albany, NY, the Pine Hills Coffee Shop, on Madison Avenue. In 1986, after extensive renovations, the coffee shop became Qualters Restaurant. The core of our breakfast, lunch and dinner menus was, with our scratch bakery on the premises, our handmade artisanal breads. The little red, pocket-size notebook of bread-makind recipes was never misplaced again.

By 1986, Qualters Restaurant had become a well-established place of hospitality, with its on-premises artisanal bakery. It became a community of people who came to be nourished and to take home a loaf of our artisanal bread to break and share with loving family and friends.

As we look back over the years, we are convinced that Qualters was meant to be. From the "come on, follow me" to the Hobart bread mixer, to Tom with his preposterous proposal, to the teacher friends of mine who invited me to their kitchen in Lake George, our future was being crafted right in front of us. All we had to say is "Let's do this." We eventually agreed, without hesitation in spite of all our fears, while not quite able to comprehend it all. We felt a deep energy to pursue this new career. We slowly acknowledged that our everyday experiences were overwhelmingly telling us this opportunity was truly meant to be.

By 1995, Qualters Restaurant, according to numerous local food critiques, became very well known for its truly caring hospitality. It excelled in a professional, creative kitchen. Its crepe-like omelets for breakfast became famous. The artisanal breads, especially honey, whole-wheat walnut bread, creative luncheon sandwiches, and full-service dinners reflected traditional and regional American and Irish cuisines. As a result, Jeanne and I were presented with many career opportunities in the hospitality, industry and the private sector.

Selling the restaurant became a major, complicated, bittersweet ongoing dialogue. In August 1995, knowing in our hearts it was in our best interests, we sold Qualters Restaurant.

The months that followed the sale were filled with new career opportunities. In the midst of all these incredible career experiences, 66 years of a deep love of bread-baking continues. I continue to make bread to this very day for my family and friends. Teaching classes in artisanal bread-making is a joy. Raising money for non-profits by teaching bread-making, and being part of a group who love bread making is a gift.

This love of making bread is due to a lifelong belief in my faith, a conviction that where there is bread there is community around a sacred table. It is also my belief that bread baking back in 1957 with my little red, bread–making notebook was the beginning, the seed, the calling that created the incredible career journey that continues today. I am still joyfully making bread. The 50-quart Hobart bread mixer holds my attention, gently forgiving me for using a 6-quart KitchenAid bread mixer. How can we not believe many of our life experiences, past, present, and future are just meant to be!

NON-FICTION

DINNER WITH PAUL NEWMAN

Pat Musick Carr

*The hero had a handsome, resolute face, kind and full of a
gentleman's grace.*

In 1990, I sat down for dinner in Groningen, the Netherlands,
in a room full of space explorers. The group of cosmonaut
and astronaut men and women had all made at least one
flight in space. I looked about me. The small girl, never
dreaming that she would one day share the making of
memories with such an illustrious group. The man who sat
on my left, my dinner partner, was the great Russian hero
who had lifted off Baikonur launch pad four times, the only
human in history to do so. Vladimir Dzhanibekov spoke
eloquent English, and so the evening flowed past us in warm
conversation. A fairy tale aura hovered about the table like a
cloud of gauze.

As dinner concluded we each took our menu cards and
gave witness to the extraordinary evening. We then passed
them to our right and around the table to be signed by
all. I took Zhani's and wrote "To the Paul Newman of
the Cosmonauts." I handed it on. When it got to the first
American wife, she looked at me and said, "You're not going
to give this to him?" "Of course, I am," I replied. When the
card arrived back to Zhani, he looked at it and then at me.
"Who is Paul Newman?" he asked. I told him that when I
got back to the United States, I would send him a videotape
of a movie titled *Butch Cassidy and the Sundance Kid* and

113

then he would know who Paul Newman is.

The next morning, we had a farewell breakfast in a Dutch windmill. The sponsors of the meeting selected six space travelers and their wives to honor and presented each woman with an armful of beautiful roses. The couples walked among the tables saying farewells. When Zhani and his wife Lydya got to my table, he put his hand on her arm and stopped her. Then taking a bud out of her bouquet, he bent down, handed me the rose, and said, "You are very beautiful." I looked into his twinkling eyes and replied, "You found out who Paul Newman is," and smiled. He laughed.

The value of travel? New cultures to know,

Geography's treasures, on us to bestow.

Person to person, making new friends

across the whole world, joy never ends.

MARTINIS AND MEMORIES

Marsha Ras

It was an early evening in May. I was sitting on the porch of an inn in Vermont with my best friend, drinking martinis and smelling the sweet smell of local pines. We both turned 75 this year. I've known her since we were six. We grew up together as neighbors, but we think of each other as sisters. She lives in Richmond and Phoenix, and I live at Shaker Pointe. Over the years we made it a point to get together, here, or there or anywhere for that matter, whenever we could. I am tickled because one of her children recently moved to Manchester, so it's a treat to see her more frequently in my part of the country.

Maybe it was the second round of martinis, or an acknowledgment of our milestone birthdays, but we took our usual reminiscing to a greater depth. At some point she asked me if I still thought about the "only child' conversation I had with my father when I was young. I responded, "you bet, how could I forget?" What follows is the recounting of that memory and a few others that in many ways shaped my destiny.

I grew up on Long Island, less than a mile from Long Island Sound. My father had an old power boat. It spent more time in dry dock than cruising around the North Shore. A day in early June, we were taking turns sanding and staining the woodwork. It was hot, even for early June, and I had already managed to varnish my leg in a few places. The boat smelled like turpentine. At one point my father asked me to sit where we could face each other.

I dearly loved my father. He died way too young. Most days when I was growing up, we behaved like brother and sister together, much to my mother's chagrin. Every once in a while, he'd say to me, "I'm putting my father hat on." This essentially meant let's stop fooling around and get serious. That always got my attention, and this was one of those times.

Apparently, my mother was having another miscarriage. This was either her fourth or fifth failed pregnancy. I never did find out the exact number. Once I was sitting next to him, he said, "Your mother is losing another baby, so It looks like you're going to be an only child for good." Before that piece of news had even sunk in, he followed with, "And if we are to have only one child, we couldn't ask for a better one than you! You are smart and funny and so curious about life that you are capable of becoming anything you want to become, if you don't kill yourself in the trying!"

I learned another life lesson at "sleepaway" camp in Vermont. My aunt and uncle owned the camp, which made it affordable. For seven weeks each summer I lived in a rustic cabin with other girls of basically the same age. We had activity periods throughout the week that included swimming lessons, riding, riflery and archery, arts and crafts, hiking, acting classes and more. I loved it there. I was a camper there on and off for four summers. In later years I became a counselor.

Every Friday evening all the campers and counselors would gather at the "theatre" to see a play being put on by the campers from a different cabin. The back of the theatre opened onto the gentle slope of the camp's mountain and provided a sweeping view of the surrounding terrain. It smelled earthy and was a great backdrop for any outdoorsy scenes.

I was in Cabin 4 this year. There were 10 girls in my cabin. After considerable discussion and compromise, we settled on the fable "The Emperor's New Clothes." We were around 10 or 11 years old at the time. We thought it was terribly funny that anyone could be convinced they were adorned in a beautiful garment when in fact they would walk the streets naked. What also cinched us choosing this fable was being able to take advantage of the outdoor backdrop for the parade scene, when most of the actors would be facing away from the audience. Everybody still expected to be nervous. It turned out that when the roles were being assigned, I wound up with the final line of the play and I would be facing the audience to deliver it.

Unfortunately, shortly before our theatre night production, I came down with a miserable cold and was sent to the infirmary. I was nasal and monotone. When my counselor came to visit and heard me talk, she said, "Would you like me to ask someone else to say your line?" I said, "No! Please help me practice the line to get it right," and she did. After more than a few tries and help with inflection and volume, I did get it right. I then asked her what the line meant. She said that since the crowd lining the parade route was totally ignoring the emperor's nakedness and not saying a word, standing up in their midst and stating the question, "Could it be that I am stupid?" would be a courageous act. She went on to explain in some detail, what having courage meant. The night of the play, I said my line with conviction and inflection and remember feeling a sense of pride in speaking the truth.

My third vignette is another camp story – more prophetic than profound. I was in shop class, not one of my favorite pastimes. We were making things out of leather. I chose to make my father a belt. I labored over this project. I used various punches to stamp his entire name in the belt plus stars, moons, and such to cover most of the entire 40+ inches of leather. The shop counselor who was, even on a good day, grumpy and certainly not a nurturer, made the following comment when he saw my finished product: "Well, I hope you can make your living with your mouth, because it's certainly not going to be with your hands!" For whatever reason, I didn't feel hurt or angry, but rather thought he was funny and more important I knew he was right.

My father wore the belt for years. He was a good sport.

So, what's been the impact of these seminal events?

On being an only child – I've tried over time to be the "eyes and ears" of the children who were never born. While still living at home I worked with my father in his lawn-spraying business, often serving in roles that a son would have typically filled. He taught me to drive one of his tractor trailers when I was 13. He needed help rearranging his fleet, so I navigated the beast in his parking lot! In school I tried various sports, some competitively, and learned to separate the role I was playing from who I was as a person. A great life lesson. Later on, I worked on and raced, or "campaigned" as we called it, a vintage MG sports car. I also mastered sailing a large sailboat and learned to ski some pretty serious terrain in the States and Europe. I've been to all seven continents, visited the 50 states and more than 60 countries. All the while I was thinking and often uttering out loud, "can you (all) see this through my eyes?"

On courage: Finding courage is the single most important takeaway and influence on my value system. I rarely make a decision without thinking about the nature of my decision-making and how it will impact me and others. I don't shy away from difficult situations and generally embrace them as learning opportunities. Personally, I've been a first responder, a hospice volunteer, and a fierce advocate for people within my sphere of influence.

Professionally, my courage lesson has had a huge impact, from working with the emotionally disturbed, early in my career, to RPI, where my administrative and academic positions required me to challenge the status quo in a male-dominated environment, and finally in my Executive and Career Coach business. I retired in 2021 after more than 25 years in private practice. Several of the seminars I particularly enjoyed delivering were "Finding Courage" and

"Fighting 101 – how to Confront Skillfully." I also worked privately with a number of executives who surprisingly just wanted an "ear" to listen to decisions they needed to make that required a courageous stance.

On using my mouth! – All three of my careers demanded strong verbal skills and the ability to say the right things at the right times. These equipped me to help children work through despair; encourage gifted engineering and science students to "leave their heads outside my classroom and enter with open hearts"; and coaching job applicants to showcase their best selves during interviews.

If I give myself the luxury of some "magical thinking," I can see myself in my role as a career coach talking to the inner girl who has shown herself here.

Career-Coach-Me – As an only child didn't you also benefit from extra attention from your parents and all that goes along with it?

Inner-Me – Yes. But, in my mind it was always overshadowed by my need to be good and do good. Sometimes people ask me if being an only child felt "special." Honestly, that never occurred to me. It always felt like a burden.

Career-Coach-Me – What else?

Inner-Me – well, by the age of 16, I worked a number of part time jobs and paid for pretty much everything but my winter coats, medical expenses and meals. I was fiercely independent.

Career-Coach-Me –Anything else? It's pretty much time to wrap this up.

Inner-Me – Yes, I'm tired too. But I have one more story to tell. It's my mother's story. And she told it often.

My first spoken word was "daddy," much to her chagrin. Thankfully, shortly thereafter I said, "mommy." But the next thing out of my mouth was a full sentence. And I've never stopped talking….

Then there is the "walking" story. One day while my mother was watching me explore my surroundings, she saw me standing and moving from chair to table and table to chair with my bottle in hand. At some point shortly thereafter, she saw me throw down the bottle and take off running down the hall. Shocked, she had to jump up and run to catch me. And I've never stopped running…

LIBATION

Pat Musick Carr

A trickle of tribute echoes the past.
Memories of ancestors pouring the last
drops onto the earth.
Libation, a prayer from deep in the heart;
A kind of thanks-giving for one to impart
in sacred spaces.

Libations have been a ritual in my family for a very long time. Originating in Mesopotamia, the symbolic act spread through North Africa and Europe, arriving in Ireland and Scotland, where it became part of my ancestry. Libations speak of tributes to the dead, success in battle, and hopes for return visits to important places. I first learned about them when a poet friend, picnicking with his family on Omaha Beach in France, poured the red liquid into the sand to honor those who lost their lives in the World War II storming of that beach.

The libations of my life form memories I often return to. They are particularly powerful reflections of precious times. They paint a picture of people and places that influenced my journey.

Yucatan jungle. Squashed into a VW bug, four of us watched gullies pour off the car. Winding down a window, Jerry held the bottle in a soaking grip and poured thanks into the wet sand.

Madrid. We sat on a stone wall across from the Prado, munching lunch. Thinking of Picasso, Goya, and Velasquez just seen, we gave libation for their gifts.

Berlin. A circle of space explorers each held a glass. Cosmonauts and astronauts, a year after the Wall came down, searched for peace and harmony on our planet.

Arkansas. A crystal-clear stream with sandy shore and a picnic shared with Nina and Slava, we poured a trickle of claret and blessed our struggle to understand the Russian language.

Idaho. A maiden balloon flight over the Salmon River. Such silent surrender to the skies! Ritually we knelt on the ground and received the libation poured upon our humbled heads.

Italy. A picnic between Roselle and Populonia, glimpsing the ancient Etruscan civilization and the Roman rebuilding atop its crown. We basked in the beauty of the sparkling sea and blessed the spirits of this sacred space.

Egypt. At dusk, a lightly blowing breeze painted the giant structures with a pale coral pigment. Power and strength filled the sky. We poured to the massive monoliths, marveling at the ingenuity, their grace.

Arkansas. A birthday celebration, 90 years. Family, dear friends gathered in a museum of American art. Love passed from one to another. An afternoon shared with the sculpture we created. In the evening, a friend offered the libation on a granddaughter's lawn.

Italy. Brolio, a castle and a winery atop the Chianti Hills, vineyards stretched to the horizon. A picnic in the garden of the enoteca and a libation poured by friends who had come all the way from Texas.

Vermont. Guns fired into the air and a folded flag rested its stars and stripes against my breast. Farewell to the precious light of life. After the service, a small luncheon of family and friends. The wine moved slowly on a downward path... to the earth returned.

Over the years we have gathered the most
special people and offered a toast
to life's love unending.
Thanks for caring, for sharing with me
the best that life can possibly be.
All gratitude sending.

NANNY

Ronnie Uss

I lived in my grandparents' house until I was almost six.

My grandmother, Bridget McNulty Kearney – who I called Nanny – was born in County Galway, in Ireland in 1874. She was the oldest of six children. Her father was the district school master, and her mother was the local postmistress. Grandpa was born in 1871 in County Mayo. His family were farmers, and he was a horse trainer.

Lured by the promise of a job at a large Pennsylvania horse farm, they made what was at that time a perilous journey across the Atlantic Ocean with their first child. No one seems to know what went awry with their plans. They ended up living in the Harlem area of New York City. There they raised six children – three boys and three girls. My mother, who was the youngest, was born when Nanny was forty-six.

Grandad became a conductor on the "L-train," the elevated railroad. He was a dapper redhead with an always-trimmed handlebar mustache. He was gentle, soft spoken and kind; had a love of music and learning; and smoked a pipe.

Nanny was a big woman. She was a head taller than Grandad. She was intelligent, progressive, practical, determined, and direct. Some found her imposing. I found her kind, soft, caring, and safe.

When she was eighteen, Mother became pregnant. She ran away from home and, guided by the local parish priest, made her way to the Foundling Home. Despite her reverence for priests and nuns, Nanny loomed over the parish priest and badgered him into revealing where her daughter was.

The day after I was born, with the adoption papers already prepared, Nanny stormed the Foundling Home and informed the indignant, protesting sister in charge: "That child comes home with us!"

My earliest memory of Nanny was of her standing by my crib. I had been frightened by the air-raid sirens. Nanny pulled aside the blackout shade so I could see the air-raid warden and understand what was happening. She stayed until I fell asleep. I remember sitting on Nanny's lap on a big chair in the parlor. I loved stroking her soft rope-veined hands and loved her sweet smell.

Nanny would feed me at the long dining room table. I was propped up on several big books. She fed me soft boiled eggs and mashed potatoes, Grandad kneeling nearby on his Prie Dieu, saying his prayers.

I was born pigeon-toed – my feet turned inward. Once I was able to walk, Nanny cleverly put my white high-top shoes on the wrong feet. That is, the right shoe on the left foot, the left shoe on the right foot. Grandad would faithfully walk me along Riverside Drive.

Nanny was kind, thoughtful, and protective of me. Once I had a dream so vivid that I remember it to this day. I dreamed that I floated down the stairs to the first floor. Mother told me it was only a dream. Nanny said it meant that I was an angel.

Nanny took me with her to early Mass every morning. One day she did not feel well. Knowing the way, I took myself – not sure if I told anyone or not. Sitting in the same pew where we always sat, I joined the others walking to the communion rail – as if I were with Nanny. The priest seemed quite taken aback upon seeing this very small child in front of him. Finally, he asked where I had studied for First Communion. Pointing next door, I confidently named the school. Somewhat reluctantly, he gave me the host.

A nosey neighbor had been sitting behind me and wasted no time in informing Nanny and all the neighbors. Mother was very concerned because the neighbors were scandalized. Nanny told her not to worry and said, "They are all hypocrites."

I'm told that Mother once took me to the third-floor bathroom to punish me for some transgression. Nanny lumbered up those long flights of stairs, broke the latch on the bathroom door, and commanded, "Don't you dare hit that child!"

When Nanny was approaching a major milestone, her adult children told her that they were going to send her back to Ireland for a visit. Nanny stood up and declared, "Ireland, I've been there. It's cold and it's damp. Send me to Bermuda instead." Of course, they did neither.

Nanny must have been a good manager. She was able to acquire their three story, greystone home on 140th street, across from City College. She also purchased AT&T stock in the early 1920's.

When Columbus Circle was being built, the residents of their condemned homes in this predominantly black neighborhood, began moving north to the Harlem area. My earliest playmates were the children of the first black family to move into this all white, Irish-Catholic neighborhood.

City College had benches by my grandparents' home. Every fair-weather day after work, Grandad would don his three-piece suit, take his pipe and sit on a bench. Frequently, one of the college professors would join him and chat. They called him "The Little Professor." One day, Mother came home from shopping and asked: "Momma, why is daddy sitting with that "colored man"? Nanny replied, "Lillian, that man has more intelligence in his little finger than all the fools in the corner bar." Nanny really was ahead of her time.

Mother remembered when she and her family would stay at a cottage on Staten Island in the summer. Nanny would sit, sifting the sand between her fingers. Looking up at the stars, she said, "Lillian, we are like a grain of sand in this vast universe." She also thought that Eleanor Roosevelt was the greatest woman of the twentieth century.

Living with my grandparents was the only real stability I was to know until I was a relatively mature adult.

Sometime after the end of World War II, my stepfather returned for good, and the five of us moved to a small house down a dirt road in the woods in Merrick, Long Island. By this time, I had a little sister and a baby brother. I don't remember any neighbors. Shortly after we moved, on my very first day of school, my baby brother was sick. So I had to walk by myself down what seemed a very long, lonely and dark dirt road to school.

We lived in Bethpage, Long Island, when my Grandad died of ALS. I was nine years old. I am told that Nanny "took to her bed" after that. We then moved to California. Nanny died when I was ten. Mother flew back to New York City with my baby sister who was too young to leave behind. I said at the time, "But I'm the only one who remembers Nanny." I was needed to help my stepfather care for my younger sister and brother. Perhaps that's when I began to feel responsible for almost everything.

We continued to move regularly and my parents' drinking progressed. By the time they were drinking compulsively, my stepfather resorted to violence more and more frequently.

I felt very guilty when I went to college in New York City and left my siblings, especially my youngest sister. She was so sweet as well as hearing-impaired. I loved her dearly. Eventually, I got married. My Uncle walked me down the aisle. For a time, my husband and I accepted the guardianship of my youngest sister to avoid her being placed in foster care.

Once Mother stopped drinking, she began to visit us, especially when things became difficult for her at home. She would just show up, laden with gifts. She could be fun and always brought things for our daughters. Just as we were getting used to her being with us, Mother would abruptly depart, as if feeling a tug on an invisible string.

After ten years of sobriety, Mother arrived intoxicated. That very night, while we were asleep, she fell. In the morning, I found blood in the bathroom, in the children's room, and where Mother slept. She was on her back, arms folded across her chest like a corpse, a ring of blood around her neck. She received 20 stitches in her scalp and was admitted to the hospital. Mother was very angry with me for having taken her there.

That night was a sleepless one. I knew Mother needed time to heal and recover before returning to my stepfather. Having worked hard to exorcize my own demons, and not wanting to expose my young daughters to the chaos, the insanity of it all, I knew Mother's staying with us was not a good option. That night while tossing in bed – aloud or to myself – I said, "Nanny, I don't know what to do." I heard her firm reply: "Oh, that one! I gave up on her years ago."

A great weight, that I did not know I was carrying, was lifted. Fortunately, my sister who had a big house near Rochester, NY, offered to have my Mother stay with her. Lilly is a lovely woman, an ER nurse, and has a spine of steel.

Mother visited us less often after that. Eventually, she and my stepfather moved to Florida. Shortly before they moved, my Mother's oldest friend confessed to her that she always thought her children would become "circus clowns," given the life we all had led.

Nanny and Grandad provided the foundation for my life. In a sense, they have always been with me as I grew up and struggled to become worthy of that heritage. They were with me as I raised my beautiful daughters – cherishing them, knowing I was gifted with their care. And when I held my newborn grandchildren. They continue to be present as I watch them grow into wonder-full people. I attribute my work ethic, enjoyment of walking, my love for music and the written word, my passion for learning, my fondness for anyone speaking with a brogue to my grandparents.

I have lived in more places, in more homes, than I can actually remember. But I can still draw the floor plan of that loving home on 140th street; still recall the phone number; and I will always remember the smell of Nanny's soap and Granddad's pipe.

And now my rope-veined hands are Nanny's.

MEMORIES

Ann Eberle

1. THE RUN-AWAY

Our friend's son, Bobby, went to Camp Chingachgook on Lake George the summer he was eight or nine. Then they got a phone call that Bobby had run away. That was frightening but, fortunately, they quickly found him walking down the road towards home.

The next time I saw Bobby I had to ask him why he had run away. As far as I knew the camp was a great place for young boys being right on the lake with a sandy beach, sailboats, tents, other boys to play with. Hard to imagine why it wouldn't have suited Bobby.

But his answer was one I never would have anticipated. Bobby had tight red curls, freckles and a surprisingly deep voice. And his answer was, "The acoustics in the dining room were atrocious!"

2. A MISS

At dinner one evening when our youngest son was a young boy I served what, to him, was the wrong thing.

"Mom!," he said. "You know I don't like Veal Farmer John!"

3. THE TRUTH

"What are you doing?" little Davie asked his father.

"I'm putting up a snow fence so the snow doesn't drift in the driveway like it did last winter."

"Da-ad, it will snow on both sides of the fence, you know."

4. GRANDMA'S SURPRISE

Three of our little granddaughters were visiting us. While I was making dinner, the girls were exploring the house.

They went upstairs for a while but suddenly reappeared in the kitchen.

"Grandma, Grandma! Come quick! There's a dead animal upstairs!"

"What is it, a mouse?" I asked.

"No! No, it's much bigger than that!"

Well obviously, I had to go upstairs and see what this could be. So up we went, the girls running ahead, giggling.

They opened the cedar chest at the foot of the guest room bed and pointed.

"See?!"

And, sure enough, there was my late mother-in-law's fur piece. The one with the head with its glass eyes and the clamp used to close its mouth on the tail. It was dead all right.

Ted Zborowski, Our neighbors at Shaker Pointe

THE WILLOW ACROSS THE ROAD

Ann M. Krupski
Photos by Ted Zborowski

Just as one person can stand out in a crowd,
so too can one tree in a field.

The graceful majesty of one willow was a landmark on Delatour Road in Latham, NY. In the mid 1960s, it was planted by Stan Lupian, the groundskeeper for the Sisters of St. Joseph of Carondelet. That beautiful tree was across the road from what has become Shaker Pointe.

For almost 60 years it stood steady through all kinds of weather. Like a guardian, it sheltered many different birds. Whenever we looked, the willow was there.

At some point, we noticed that it was not as full as it used to be. We saw the stately willow diminish as storms and climate change weakened it. A lightning strike felled one large section. After yet another damaging storm in 2021, it had to be taken down.

But the willow still lives. The remaining stump has sprouted *new life*.

CREATIVE ELDERS

CHAPTER FOUR

Reflections

TREE OF LIFE: Sung Ae Lim

Barbara Mazur, "Reflections"

IN MEMORIAM

Ann M. Krupski

In memory of all those who touched our lives.

Feelings roam freely within us:
catch us by surprise – at times;
inform us of our love;
accentuate our losses;
allow us to grieve and to cry;
stretch our hearts beyond our mind's limitations;
and create the space in which compassion matures –
changing us forever.

TOGETHER

Ronnie Uss

Living in an elder community,
    we see aging
    writ large.

We experience
    the opportunities,
    the blessings,
    the joys,
    TOGETHER.

We learn and grow.
    We laugh and play.
    We cry and mourn.
    TOGETHER.

We see
    more ambulances,
    attend more wakes,
    go to more funerals,
    TOGETHER.

Living with 200 or more friends,
> we share more experiences
> from joy to sorrow,
> and receive more caring and support.

As the poet Rumi said:
> "We're all just
> > walking each other
> > home."

What an honor
> to walk
> each other
> HOME.

What a privilege
> to be
> walked
> HOME.

CONNECTIONS
Ann M. Krupski

Somewhere

  there must be an invisible root system

  connecting us all,

  wrapping around our hearts tenderly.

Sometimes

  we feel a spontaneous,

  shared warmth with another.

A wonderful, exhilarating surprise –

That gift

  moves us

  to the blessing of a genuine, broad smile.

And maybe a cup of tea –

DANCING

Ronnie Uss

Each morning
        the sun "rises" and the moon "sets;"
Each evening, the moon "rises" and sun "sets."

During each year,
        the rising and setting move
        back and forth across the horizon:
A slow-motion, predictable
        planetary dance.

Intellectually, we all know
        the earth rotates around the sun,
        revolves around the moon.

Perhaps, if we are silent and very still,
        we can almost "feel" the
        imperceptible movement of the earth.

(Continued next page)

Too often, we act as if
　　　　we are the center,
　　　　as if the world rotates and
　　　　revolves around us.

In reality, we rotate and revolve
　　　　around each other,
　　　　sometimes in light and
　　　　sometimes in darkness.
　　　　Sometimes shined upon
　　　　sometimes shining upon others.

We are intimately interconnected
　　　　and interdependent
　　　　rotating and revolving
　　　　in this complex, delicate
　　　　dance of life.

MOMENTS

Ann M. Krupski

Every moment contains
a history of all moments:
days —
        hours, minutes,
           experiences
wrapped in stillness soaking the soul.
Each moment
reaches inward
        and outward,
coloring time
as if it were a page in an unwritten book,
touching the heart
in myriad ways,
prompting cues of awakening —
Now
is
beyond time.
Focused attention
stops
the clock.

NOW

Ronnie Uss

Time is an artificial construct,
    a convenience that facilitates
    our lives together.

In reality, it is always now,
    always the present moment.

And yet, we spend a lot of our "time,"
    ruminating about the past or
    fantasizing about the future.

We act as if we are swimming
    in an endless ocean of "time",
    while we paddle in our puddle
    past all our nows.

Our minds constantly emit commentary –

    judgments, grievances, cravings –

    that separate us from the present moment,

    ourselves, and from each other.

Like the Wizard of Oz,

    our minds project a story

    in which we are the protagonist –

    hero or victim in turn.

Without being present in our lives,

    we are pale actors

    in a home movie.

Living in the present moment

    is our super power.

NATURE'S SYMPHONY

Ann M. Krupski

The sounds of nature can delight us. So many
different "instruments" in an amazing orchestra.
LISTEN

clear, high tones of cardinals
familiar melodies of robins
soft cooing of mourning doves

varied repertoire of mockingbirds
emphatic honking of geese as they move
into formation
cock-a-doodle-doo of a rooster
greeting dawn

buzzing of bees as they gather pollen
a softer buzz-like hum as a
hummingbird approaches or
leaves a feeder

shrill sounds of shorebirds
      rolling crescendo of waves

wind rushing through trees
      skipping and scattering leaves

quieter evening sounds of crickets and tree frogs
      penetrating w h o o from an owl at night

silent measures after a snowfall
      percussive pitter patters of rain
      bass drum booms of thunder

All these sounds
enter our ears
and then our hearts

LISTEN

WALKING THROUGH TIME THAT ISN'T

Laurie Musick Wright

To be like a mystic
I walk through time that isn't
searching for the eternity of love

each step appears surreal
like a world of opposites
quiet and loud, smooth and rough, light and dark

embracing each moment with resolve
to just be present
alert and contemplative

breathing in a sense of grace
smelling a magnolia blossom
tracing a labyrinth of rose petals

resonating in perfect harmony
a crescendo of clashing cymbals
sound waves vibrating into eternity

To be like a mystic
I hold space for myself and others
on this journey called life

where the sun warms me
water quenches my thirst
and plants nourish every cell

arriving with an open heart
soaking up love like a sponge
ringing it out to anoint another

feeling this love within my soul
in every cell
in every breath

deep feelings transferred without words
exchanging an indescribable love
a massive all-encompassing blanket

in this present moment
I am here, now
in the eternity of love

WHO?

Ronnie Uss

Our minds are a complex marvel –
    the repository of upbringing,
    experiences, learning,
    acquired preferences and proclivities.

We act as if our thoughts are real –
    not merely projections
    of our biased mind.

We develop habits, patterns of
    thinking that reinforce
    our biases and prejudices.

We speak our mind-generated
    audio book thoughts,
    live by them, act on them.

We empower them
    by coupling them
    with our emotions.

We presume that our mind
    is at the epicenter of
    our being
    and is in control.

We do not have to be
    at the mercy
    of such an unreliable autocrat.

Our minds are only a tool.
    We have the ability
    to shape them,
    to sharpen or dull them,
    if we choose.

A four year old niece
    was asked by her aunt
    if she would like to go
    for ice cream.

She responded:
"I am not the boss of me.
You have to ask my Mom."

Ask yourself:
    "Who is the boss of me?" **WHO?**

TURN ORDINARY WORKS INTO AN EXTRAORDINARY EXISTENCE

Laurie Musick Wright

Thoughts of doubt block the energy
of what craves to be born

Screaming to be heard through
disregard

Yearning to express in a mind distracted
with obstructive chatter

Searching for moments of stillness to make way for the heart

Harmonizing in the mystery of what will become

Willing to be present in the birthing of the new

Extraordinary gifts emerging from the forgotten self

Praying for the creative unfoldment of inner beauty

A new way. A new life. A new being.

A CROWD OF GIFTS
Ann M. Krupski

Each day is a crowd of gifts available endlessly.

One cold blue sky day in March,
a small bird sat on a telephone wire.
Its energetic movements
caught my attention.
My curiosity alert, I prolonged watching.
That small bird's entire body
moved with definite determination –
bending down,
           then stretching up.
Down again
           and up again
Over and over – tirelessly.

Before it flew away, I quietly smiled with realization.
           Closed windows
           blocked March cold and outdoor sounds,
           but not surprise.
That bird was singing!
An unusual gift received:
           A bird song
           SEEN.

HIDDEN SANCTUARY
Ann M.Krupski

Within each of us
is an ever-present,
heart centered space.
Its presence is a sturdy, felt reality
of enduring availability.

During times of contemplation or creativity,
we are more aware of its activity
flowing through us.
In those sacred moments,
we are no longer the player
but have become an instrument.
A wondrous,
      mysterious gift.

When we pay attention,

this gift finds us awake.

When we have a new idea,

this amazing gift is already enlivened.

When we put energy into a project,

this incredible mystery

      works as our partner –

      prodding, leading, guiding.

Some call this gift inspiration,

others creativity.

When naming dissolves,

essence prevails and

revelation is recognized:

      A hidden sanctuary

      filled with the vibrancy

      of indestructible L I G H T

      shines BRILLIANTLY within us.

AGING

Ann M. Krupski

We become like seasoned mountain climbers
climbing mountains
without a map.

What we don't know
becomes an entrance
to brave new encounters with:
who we really are,
what really matters, and how we will travel
this as yet unique, uncharted route.

No longer a stranger
to receiving surprising updates,
unpredictability greets us at every turn.

As we gain solid
or even shaky footing
on this engaging adventure,
the body-mind-heart secures the wisdom
needed to proceed.

BEATING HEART

Mary Ann Lettau

I should like it
If consciousness
Lived on after death.

I'm curious-
What will happen
    to kids and friends,
    people I know,
    people I don't.

Dystopia?
Paradise found?

But would I care
Without a beating heart?

HAVE YOU EVER . . .

Ann Eberle

Have you felt this
That you're about
A half step removed
From life as it was

Have you seen this
All of nature is
Beautiful but about
A half step removed
From your experience now

Have you found this
That food is still tasty
But you really don't
Need as much anymore
As you once did

Have you been missing
People with whom you once

Shared love and caring
And experiences
Close family and friends

Have you been recalling
Homes where you and yours
Once lived, celebrated in
Slept in, felt safe and
Comfortable inside

Do your days sort of
Ring hollow, ending
While you're trying to
Know what you should
Be doing

?

NO CHOICE

Mary Ann Lettau

As my connection to the world
Becomes more tenuous,
The hold it has on me
Becomes stronger.

I said once on a lovely day,
"I do not want to die."
(so much beauty and song!)
The world replied, "No choice."

A LOVE NOTE

Laurie Musick Wright

You are present within a love most high

Know that you are...
    loved and held in Grace
    capable and strong
    free of stagnation, flowing like a stream
    full of goodness to share with family, friends,
      and coworkers
    blessed with a heart full of love
    safe and sound in an everlasting light
    a unique creation of love itself
    a perfect child of creative, divine love

Know that...
    your desires are an expression of creative source
    your greatest gifts are meant to be shared
    you will be given what you ask for from your heart
    only you can create what is for you most meaningful
      to share
    you can change what is most challenging for you
    your greatest challenge will bring about your
      greatest reward
    love is your strength in all things
    you can fully trust this love.

METTA MEDITATION *(loving kindness intention)*

Mary Ann Lettau

For myself:

      May I enjoy good health until I die.

      May I grow in wisdom, gratitude, and patience.

      May I love more completely.

For immediate family and closest friends:

      May you find a safe and secure place in this world.

      May you have what you need.

      May you live with love.

For my fellow humans:

      May you be free of pestilence and war.

      May you be free of oppression and prejudice.

      May your talents nourish our world,

           the only home we know.

For our natural world and its flora and fauna:

      May you enjoy clean air and water in

           which to flourish.

      May your beauty and uniqueness be a blessing.

      May the human species see the mutual need

           and interconnectedness of all living beings.

Laurie Musick Wright, "Provincial House, Latham, NY — Peace"

Contributors

TREE OF LIFE: Mary Ann Lettau

Fran Berg | 95

Stephanie Bollam | 78

Pat Musick Carr | 96

Lisa Cirillo | 80

Jane Comerford | 75

Barbara Donnaruma | 83

Ann Eberle | 87

Carole Egan | 80

Jack Egan | (1942-2021)

Polly Ginsberg | 81

Cathy Kruegler | 72

Ann Krupski | 80

Sung Ae Lim | 86

Mary Ann Lettau | 77

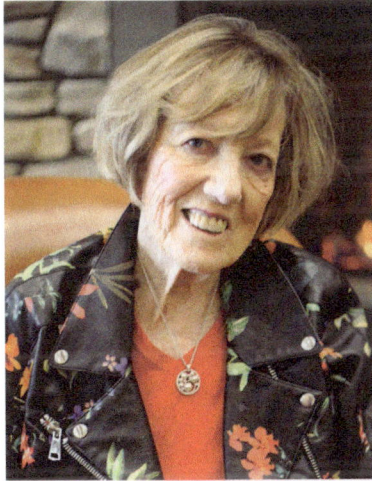

Barbara Mazur | 78

Jean Padula | 84

John Pattison | 93

Vincent Powers | 91

Harold Qualters | 84

Marsha Ras | 75

Nancy Scarchilli | 72

Dick Shirey | 80

Eileen Shirey | 78

Janet Troidle | 79

Ronnie Uss | 83

Charla Whimple | 76

Laurie Musick Wright | 69

Ted Zborowski | 91

Acknowledgments

TREE OF LIFE: *Carole Egan*

The June 2022 Writing Workshop with Paul Grondahl, Director of the New York State Writers Institute at the University at Albany, was a great success. Residents deep dived into the art of the written word, drawing from their own experiences. Shaker Pointe tells the tale of transfiguration as residents have creative opportunities to grow and express themselves in the community on a daily basis.

ACKNOWLEDGMENTS

This book started as an idea to encourage residents of the Shaker Pointe community to write and publish what they wrote. Administration received the suggestion with great enthusiasm. Executive Director, **Kathy Welden** and our former Director of Operations, **Katelyn Dwyer** have remained solidly committed and entirely supportive. Their consistent encouragement and robust confidence in residents' abilities have been invaluable and greatly appreciated.

Pat Musick Carr, Barbara Donnaruma, Ann Eberle, Ann Krupski, and **Mary Ann Lettau** gathered together because they are keenly interested in writing. Their ideas and suggestions were extremely valuable.

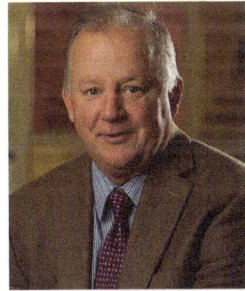

Paul Grondahl inspired us at the writing workshop he gave in June 2022. He encouraged us with his thorough reviews of writings that seven of us had sent to him. We remain immensely grateful for his vibrant approach to the skills involved in writing. He has been a valued supporter of our writing efforts. How fortunate we are to have such a skilled, accomplished, award-winning journalist and biographer who as a mentor is genuinely interested in our writing. Paul is currently the Director of the New York State Writers Institute at the University at Albany.

A committee was formed to review all manuscripts submitted for consideration in our book. **Ken Harris,** a Shaker

Pointe Board Member who has been involved in senior communities his entire career; **Joanne St. Hilaire,** a Sister of St. Joseph of Carondelet, who taught American literature and writing at the college level; and **Bernadette Verdile,** a resident with editing experience. This committee of three spent numerous hours together reviewing submissions. We are thankful for their gift of time and careful reviews.

Beverly McGuinness refreshed her typing and computer skills. She gave countless hours of her time. Beverly was not only skilled and competent but also magnanimous and patient. Our time together led to much laughter and enduring friendship.

There are many benefits to living in a community like Shaker Pointe. **Laurie Musick Wright** is one such treasure. Laurie is a wonderful writer and also a professional graphic designer. This book has benefited from her multiple skills and gifts, including her dedication to beauty and excellence.

Stephanie Bollam gracefully shared her skills as a retired copy editor who has also taught copy editing. She faithfully applied her well-honed abilities to offer editing suggestions for the final drafts.

Eleanor Doyle graciously reviewed the final drafts. She is a retired English teacher and supervisor of test construction and analysis with the NYS Department of Education and Civil Service.

Noreen Powell is our popular, gifted and well respected art teacher. Her guidance results in amazing resident artwork.

Many residents contributed their illustrations of the Tree of Life created in an art class. Renderings by **Carole Egan, Polly Ginsburg, Sung Ae Lim, Mary Ann Lettau, Nancy Scarchilli,** and **Charla Wimple** are featured on the chapter title pages. **Jack Egan** *(1942-2021)* painted the Tree of Life featured on the book cover.

Barbara Mazur contributed her watercolor depicting a scene reflected in a pond.

Ted Zborowski's photographs captured nature scenes found around Shaker Pointe.

Most of all, we are grateful to all of our authors. Some made a courageous commitment to give voice to their memories and were willing to share their stories. Many designed descriptive word combinations to paint seasonal or personal pictures. A few worked with the joy, challenges and the power of rhymes. All were inspired by imagination and simply trusted its endless expressions.

Our authors' inspired and determined efforts made CREATIVE ELDERS possible.

*Laurie Musick Wright, a panoramic view of
Shaker Pointe at Carondelet, from the hill.*

ACKNOWLEDGMENTS